**Chloe Michaels on the
pleasures and perils of internet romance:**

Advantages of a virtual boyfriend:

1. They always listen when you talk.

2. They don't judge you.

3. Sweatpants and bad hair? Don't care.

4. You can't ever really get hurt.

Disadvantages of a virtual boyfriend:

1. They can't keep you warm at night.

The more time I spend with Lieutenant Thane Carter, the more I appreciate my online friend, DifferentDrummer. Thane thinks he knows everything, and he drives me crazy. DifferentDrummer really "gets" me. There's only one problem: he's not here...

Or is he?

* * *

**AMERICAN HEROES:
They're coming home—and finding love!**

Dear Reader,

"Are your books autobiographical?" I usually answer this question by saying bits and pieces of my real life make it into each book, and that's absolutely true. The Texas Rescue series takes place in Austin, for example, which is where I met and dated my husband. The Doctors MacDowell series drew on situations I experienced during the years I spent in hospitals and doctors' offices in my previous career in the medical industry.

But this book?

Like the heroine of this book, I graduated from West Point, I was stationed in Texas and I was an army officer in the Military Police Corps, where I pulled thirty-six-hour shifts like she does. Is this book autobiographical? Honestly, the answer is still no. I married a civilian Texan, for starters!

Lieutenant Chloe Michaels is not me, but is she somebody real? Yes. She is everybody real who I knew at West Point and in the US Army. She is a mosaic, a million bits and pieces of different people and personalities and experiences from which I drew a new character, a woman who I think deserves a happily-ever-after kind of love. I hope you will think so, too, when you finish the last page and close the book.

I'd love to hear what you think. You can email me through my website at www.carocarson.com, or post a comment on Facebook. I'm at www.Facebook.com/authorcarocarson.

Cheers,

Caro Carson

The Lieutenants' Online Love

Caro Carson

HARLEQUIN® SPECIAL EDITION

Recycling programs
for this product may
not exist in your area.

ISBN-13: 978-1-335-46576-4

The Lieutenants' Online Love

Copyright © 2018 by Caroline Phipps

Printed in U.S.A.

Despite a no-nonsense background as a West Point graduate, army officer and Fortune 100 sales executive, **Caro Carson** has always treasured the happily-ever-after of a good romance novel. As a RITA® Award–winning Harlequin author, Caro is delighted to be living her own happily-ever-after with her husband and two children in Florida, a location that has saved the coaster-loving theme-park fanatic a fortune on plane tickets.

Visit the Author Profile page at Harlequin.com for more titles.

This book is dedicated to the women of West Point,

the ones who came before me, especially the Class of '80, who first proved we belonged,

the ones who lived it with me, especially Chriss, who dragged me off post to have fun in Alabama, Texas and Panama, and Gill, who can make me laugh even while we're doing push-ups in a sawdust pit at Airborne School,

and the ones who continue the Long Gray Line after me, especially 1LT Bethany Leadbetter, who so patiently answered this Old Grad's questions about today's service—and who is proof that the US Army has the country's best and brightest in its ranks.

Beat Navy.

Chapter One

Today, I was desperate for tater tots.

Chloe stared at her blinking cursor, her finger hovering over the enter key on her laptop. One second, not even that, was all it would take for that sentence to be sent to him, no way to take it back. Would he think she was dumb or would he think she was funny?

It shouldn't matter. The man was no more than a series of words on a screen, a modern-day pen pal. She wrote to him with BallerinaBaby as her user name. He wrote back as DifferentDrummer. A freebie conversation app had matched them up months ago and they'd been writing back and forth ever since, but Chloe knew that wasn't the same as being real friends in real life.

It shouldn't matter, but it did. She wanted to make him laugh. Something about his notes lately made her think her anonymous correspondent had been having a hard week. He had talked to her through all the crazy months she'd been bouncing from one place to another. He'd listened to all her thoughts and worries and hopes. It was the least she could do to help him out if he was tired and overworked. Friends and lovers ought to take care of each other. Chloe believed emotional support was just as important as physical compatibility in a relationship, so—

Chloe snatched her finger away from the enter key. She was looking at nothing more than the basic white screen of an outdated app, yet she was worrying about emotional parity in a relationship. She needed to keep the proper perspective on this…this…whatever it was.

What should she call it when her digital pen pal felt like a better friend than the living human beings around her? Borderline insanity?

She didn't know any of the human beings around her, that was the problem. She didn't know anyone in the entire state of Texas. She was newly arrived in a new town for a new job. All her stuff was still in boxes. The only constant was her pen pal. She didn't want him to think she was dumb, because if she lost him, too…well, she'd lose the most reliable presence in her life for these last five months.

Her cursor was still blinking. *Tots.*

Tater tots. Was that what she was going to talk about? She was going to talk about tots when what she was honestly feeling was lonely?

"Roger that," she said out loud, and hit Enter.

The alarm on her wristwatch went off. Time to get ready for work.

Chloe carried her laptop with her and set it by her bathroom sink so she could keep an eye on the screen. If Different Drummer was online, he would answer immediately. It was one of the things she loved about him. She smoothed her hair back and twisted it into the low, tight bun that she was required to wear every day.

Her cursor blinked in silence.

Tots!

Men didn't really joke about food cravings, at least not the men in her world, and there were plenty of men in her world. They talked about women, especially their breasts, and they talked about drinking, especially beer, but they didn't joke about food cravings.

The cursor kept blinking.

Food cravings. What had she been thinking?

She'd probably, finally scared off Different Drummer. There were so many jokes about women and food cravings, he might think she was confessing some kind of hormonal thing, a craving like pregnant women were supposed to get. Worse, maybe he thought it was a monthly craving. Guys were so squeamish about things like that. A definite turnoff.

She hadn't been trying to turn him off. She hadn't been

trying to turn him on, either. It wasn't like anyone could seduce a man with a line about tater tots.

She jabbed a few extra bobby pins into her bun. Seduce him. Ha. She didn't even know what he looked like. The simple little app didn't have the capacity to send photos. She scowled at her reflection in the mirror. With her hair pulled back tightly, her face devoid of any makeup—she'd just sweat it off at work, anyway—she didn't look like any kind of seductress.

She pulled a sports bra over her bun carefully, then wrestled the rest of the way into it. Good thing she was flexible. It was the kind of bra that didn't let anything show, even when she was soaked in sweat, the kind of bra that kept a girl as flat as possible, because bouncy curves were frowned on in her profession.

She pulled on her comfy, baggy pants and zipped up her matching jacket, checking her laptop's screen between each article of clothing.

He had to be offline. If he was online, he would have answered her…unless he was turned off by a ballerina who was obsessed with tater tots. Which she wasn't.

She yanked on her best broken-in boots. If there was anything she needed to stop obsessing over, it was him, the mystery man who always seemed to get her sense of humor, who always seemed as happy to chat with her all night as she was to chat with him. It was too easy to forget it was all an illusion. She wasn't really Ballerina Baby; he wasn't really a unique man who marched to the beat of a Different Drummer, a mystery man who sent her long notes and found himself hopelessly charmed by her words.

Was he?

Today, I was desperate for tater tots.

Blink, blink.

Nope. He wasn't hopelessly charmed. It was time for Ballerina Baby to join the real world.

Her fingertips had just touched the laptop screen, ready to close it before leaving her new apartment, when a sentence in blue magically appeared.

You crack me up.

He got it. She'd made him laugh. Mission accomplished.

The next blue sentence appeared: Or am I not supposed to laugh? The word desperate sounds rather...

Desperate? she typed one-handed. Then she stuffed her wallet in her pocket, but not her car keys. She knew from experience that if she started chatting to Different Drummer, she'd lose track of time and forget that she had to be somewhere. She bit down on the metal ring of her key fob, holding it in her teeth to leave two hands free for typing. She wouldn't forget about work as long as she had her car keys in her teeth.

Another blue line appeared on-screen. They say most men lead lives of quiet desperation.

Chloe raised one eyebrow. They slipped in famous quotes now and then, just to see if the other person would identify the quote, their own little nerdy game. This one was no challenge. How very Thoreau of you. (Too easy.)

He replied, You, however, are not like most men. (I knew it was easy.)

For starters, I'm a woman. Her words showed up in hot pink as she typed—the app's choice for female users, not hers.

He sent her a laughing-face emoji. I was thinking more along the lines that you don't seem to lead a quiet life. You also never sound desperate. I don't think you'd be quiet about it if you were.

She was typing while holding car keys in her teeth. Quietly desperate? He didn't know the half of it.

Were you able to procure the tots? Tell me you did it noisily.

Shamelessly. I bought a big bag of frozen tots at the grocery store a couple of hours ago. They didn't survive long.

You killed them already? All of them?

All of them. A one-pound bag.

Blink, blink.

For a moment, just one tiny, insecure moment, she worried again that she'd turned him off. Ballerina Baby didn't sound like the kind of woman who would eat a whole bag of tater tots at one sitting, did she? The next second, impatient with all these self-doubts, she sucked in a faintly metallic breath around her key ring and shoved aside all the insecurity. This was her friend—yes, her friend—and sometimes a pause was just a pause.

I've shocked you into silence with my brutal killing of a bag of tots, haven't I?

Not at all. I'm deciding how best to advise you so that you won't be tried for murder. I don't think they'd let you write to me from jail. I'd miss you.

Chloe's fingers fell silent. He'd miss her, and he wasn't afraid to say it. He was so different from all the other men she knew. So much better. Would he find it weird if she suddenly switched gears and wrote that?

Instead, she wrote: If I hadn't killed them all, they would have sat in my freezer, taunting me, testing my willpower. No, they needed to die. 'twere best to be done quickly.

Very Lady Macbeth of you. (Too easy.)

Yes, well, unlike Lady McB, I ate all the evidence. I guess I shouldn't feel too superior. In order to eat her evidence, she would have had to eat the king's guards. Rather filling, I'd imagine.

He had a quick comeback. If Macbeth had been about cannibalism, English class would have been much more interesting.

Ha. She smiled around the car keys in her mouth. At any rate, 'tis done. Half with mustard, half with ketchup, all with salt.

Then you're safe. We can keep talking. How was the rest of your day?

If only the last guy she'd seriously dated had been so open about saying he liked her. If only any guy she'd ever dated had been like Different Drummer.

But the car keys in her teeth did their job. They were getting heavy; she had to go.

I wish I could stay and chat, but I gotta run. And then, just in case he thought she was an unhealthy glutton, she added, Time to go burn off a whole bagful of tater calories. Talk to you tomorrow.

There. That didn't sound desperate or obsessed or…in love. She couldn't fall in love with a man she'd never met.

Looking forward to it, Baby.

But if they broke their unwritten rule and arranged to meet in real life…

The alarm on her wristwatch sounded again.

If they met in real life, he'd find out she was no ballerina—not that she'd ever said she was, but she'd never made it clear she wasn't. She certainly wasn't the kind of woman who was any guy's baby. Most guys were a little intimidated by her, something it had taken her a few years to realize.

But with him? She could show so many more sides of herself. The soft side, the insecure side, the side that worried about making friends, and yes, the side that adored the ballet. A lot of pop psychology criticized the digital age for enabling everyone to pretend to be someone they were not while they were online, but Chloe felt like this situation was the opposite. The anonymity let her be her whole self with Drummer, not only her work self. She'd be crazy to mess with a good thing. She'd follow the rules, and not try to figure out who he really was.

She picked up the last item she always wore for work, her patrol cap. The way she slid the camouflage cap over her hair, the way she pulled the brim down just so, were second nature to her. The cap was well broken-in; she'd been wearing this exact one throughout her four years as a cadet at West Point, the United States Military Academy.

Although she was so familiar with her uniform that she could dress in the dark in a matter of seconds when required, Chloe checked the mirror to be sure her uniform would pass inspection, as she'd been trained to do. The American flag on her shoulder and the name *Michaels* embroidered over her pocket were the same as they'd been since she'd first raised her right hand as a new cadet at the military academy and sworn to defend the Constitution.

The embroidered gold bar on the front of her hat was new. She'd graduated in May, so now she owed the US Army five years of service in return for her bachelor's degree. She was going to serve those years in her first choice of branch, the Military Police Corps. She was a second lieutenant now, the lowest rank of commissioned officers, but she was a commissioned officer with all the responsibility and authority that entailed. After four years of West Point in New York, three weeks of Airborne School in Georgia and four months of military police training at Fort Leonard Wood, Missouri, she was ready to lead her first platoon of MP soldiers here in Texas. So ready.

Tonight, she'd be riding along in a patrol car with the officer on duty, the first of a few mandatory nights familiarizing herself with the post she'd call home for the next three or four years. Once she knew her way around the streets of Fort Hood, she'd take shifts as the officer on duty herself, the highest-ranking MP during the midnight hours, the one who had to make the final decisions—and the one who had to accept the blame if anything went wrong.

First impressions were important. After West Point, Air Assault School, Airborne School and Military Police Basic Officer Leadership Course, Chloe knew exactly what was expected of her. She looked at the officer in the mirror and wiped the smile from her face. She could be Ballerina Baby tomorrow, cozying up to her Different Drummer and being as soft and girly as she liked.

In private.

Tonight, it was time for Second Lieutenant Chloe Michaels to go be a badass.

First Lieutenant Thane Carter was done being a badass—at least for the next twelve hours.

He was almost home. His apartment building was visible through his windshield. He kept moving on autopilot, parking his Mustang, getting out, grabbing his long-empty coffee mug and locking the car. He put on his patrol cap, an automatic habit whenever he was outdoors in uniform, pulling the brim down just so, and headed for his building, a three-story, plain beige building, identical to the five other buildings clustered around the apartment complex's outdoor swimming pool.

His primary objective for the next twelve hours was to get sleep, and a lot of it, ASAP—as soon as possible. Perhaps he'd wake up after a few hours and have a pizza delivered to his door later tonight, but then he'd go right back to sleep until dawn.

At dawn, he'd get up, put on a fresh uniform and return to duty at Fort Hood, where he was both the senior platoon leader and the acting executive officer in a military police company. That MP company, the 584th MP Company to be exact, was currently short one platoon leader, and Thane was feeling the pain.

There were normally four platoon leaders in the company, each officer in charge of roughly thirty enlisted personnel. Most of the year, MPs trained for their wartime missions, the same as every other kind of unit stationed stateside, rehearsing likely scenarios, keeping up their qualifications on their weapons. But MPs were unique: roughly one month out of every three, they pulled garrison duty.

Fort Hood was a sizable town, a military installation where sixty thousand soldiers and civilians worked and where tens of thousands lived with their families. Garrison duty required MPs to perform the functions of a regular civilian police department, patrolling Fort Hood in police cruisers as they did everything from traffic control to answering 911 calls. During that month, one of the four platoon leaders was always on duty as the officer in charge of law enforcement.

Except there weren't four platoon leaders at the moment, only three. Covering the night and weekend shifts among just three lieutenants meant that each of them was pulling a thirty-six-hour shift every third day. Officers didn't get the next day off after working all night. Thane had worked Monday, then Monday night straight on through until Tuesday evening. That thirty-six hours had been followed by twelve hours off to sleep, hit the grocery store, get his uniform ready for the next day. Wednesday would be a straightforward twelve-hour day, but getting sleep Wednesday night was critical, because Thursday morning would start another thirty-six-hour shift straight through to Friday evening.

The schedule was taking its toll. Law enforcement was important work. Necessary work. But after living the MP motto, Assist-Protect-Defend, for thirty-six hours straight, Thane was ready to assist himself right into the sack.

Alone.

To sleep.

He was single. Never married, no current girlfriend, not even dating. No surprise there. He'd worked—what? Thane counted it up in his head as he trudged from his parking space toward his mailbox, each step heavy with exhaustion. Twelve, twelve, thirty-six, twelve…hell, he'd only had twenty-four consecutive hours off one time in the past week, and it had been that way for weeks now. They really needed to fill that fourth platoon leader slot.

More downtime would help his sleep, but it wouldn't help his love life. Having no time to date was only half the reason he didn't have a woman in his life.

The other half was the scarcity of women with whom he could spend that precious downtime. The US Army was an overwhelmingly male space. Maybe 15 percent of all soldiers were women, but even so, the female MPs in his unit were off-limits. Whether he outranked them or they outranked him, dating someone within the same unit was a military offense, damaging to good order, discipline and authority, according to regulations, and grounds for a court-martial. Thane didn't need a regulation to keep him from temptation there, anyway. In the Brotherhood of Arms, the women he trained and served with were brothers-in-arms, too. Teammates, not dates. Half of them were married, anyway, which put them off-limits by Thane's personal code.

Of course, there were other servicewomen, single servicewomen, stationed at Fort Hood who were in units and positions that were completely unrelated to his, but there were roadblocks there, as well. Dating between an enlisted soldier and an officer was forbidden. Period. That knocked a couple of thousand women at Fort Hood right out of the dating pool. Since Thane was a commissioned officer, he could only date another commissioned officer who was not in his unit, but he rarely had a chance to meet female officers who worked in different branches of the army—that whole working thirty-six hours every third day had a lot to do with that. The police worked Saturdays and Sundays. And nights. And holidays.

Thane's brother, still living back home in South Carolina, was head over heels for a woman he'd met at work, one of his clients. But Thane's only "clients" were women who called 911 for help. Victims. Or they were women on the other side of that coin—not victims, but perpetrators. Two of the soldiers in his platoon had served a warrant on a woman suspected of check forgery today. Or was that yesterday? The days were all becoming one blur.

The odds of him meeting a datable woman at work were pretty much zero out of a million. Thane would've shaken his head in disgust, but that would've taken too much energy. One foot in front of the other, trudging past the apartment complex's swimming pool, that was all he had the energy for.

Building Six's mailboxes were grouped together in the stairwell. So were several of his male neighbors, all checking their mail at the same time, all in the same uniform Thane wore. At least one person in every apartment here was in the service. Everyone left Fort Hood after the American flag had been lowered for the day and everyone arrived home around the same time, an army rush hour. Everyone checked their mail before disappearing behind their apartment doors. They were all living off post in a civilian apartment complex, but the military influence of Fort Hood was impossible to escape in the surrounding town of Killeen.

As Thane used a key to open his little cubby full of two days' worth of junk mail, he exchanged greetings with the other men. To be more accurate, Thane exchanged silent lifts of the chin, the same acknowledgment he'd been exchanging with guys since the hallowed halls of high school. That had

been eight years ago, but still, that was the level of close-
ness the average guy reached with the average guy. A lift of
the chin. A comment on a sports team, perhaps, during the
NFL playoffs or Game Five of the World Series. Maybe, if
he saw someone at the mailboxes whom he hadn't seen in
a while, they might acknowledge each other with a lift of
the chin and actually speak. "You back from deployment?"

The answer was usually a shrug and a *yeah*, to which the
answer was a nod and a *yeah, thought so, hadn't seen you
around in a while,* followed by each guy retreating to his
apartment, shutting a door to seal himself off from the hundreds of others in the complex, hundreds of people roughly
Thane's age and profession, all living in the same place.

He had no one to talk to.

Thane started up the concrete stairs to his apartment, each
boot landing as heavily as if it were made of concrete, too.

He lived on the third floor, a decision he regretted on
evenings like this one. Thane hit the second-story landing.
One more flight, and he could fall in bed. As he rounded
the iron banister, an apartment door opened. A woman his
age appeared in the door, her smile directed down the stairs
he'd just come up. Another man in uniform was coming up
them now, a man who wouldn't be sleeping alone.

"Hi, baby," the man said.

"You're home early," the woman said, sounding like that
was a wonderful gift for her. "How was your day?"

"You won't believe this, but the commander decided—"
The door closed.

Thane slogged his way up to his floor.

Bed. All he wanted was his own bed, yet now he couldn't
help but think it would be nice not to hit the sheets alone. He
had an instant mental image of a woman in bed with him. He
couldn't see her face, not with her head nestled into his
shoulder, but he could imagine warm skin and a happy, interested voice, asking *How was your day?* They'd talk, two
heads on one pillow.

Pitiful. What kind of fantasy was that for a twenty-six-year-old man to have? He was heading to bed without a woman, but it wasn't sex he was lonely for. Not much, anyway. He wanted someone to talk to, someone waiting to talk to him, someone who cared what he thought after days full of people who broke laws, people who were hurt, people who were angry.

Better yet, he wanted someone to share a laugh with.

He scrubbed a hand over the razor stubble that he'd be shaving in less than twelve hours to go back to work. Yeah, he needed a laugh. There was nothing to laugh at around here.

His phone buzzed in his pocket—two shorts and a long, which meant he had a message waiting in his favorite app. The message had to be from his digital pen pal. The app had paired him up months ago with someone going by Ballerina Baby. He didn't know anything about her, not even her real name, and yet, she was someone with whom he did more than nod, someone to whom he said something meaningful once in a while. He could put his thoughts into words, written words in blue on a white screen. He got words back from her, hot pink and unpredictable, making him feel more connected to the woman behind them than he felt to anyone else around here.

Thane took the last few stairs two at a time. He wanted to get home. He had twelve hours ahead to sleep—but not alone. There was someone waiting to talk to him, after all.

He unlocked the door and walked into his apartment, tossing his patrol cap onto the coffee table with one hand as he jerked down the zipper of his uniform jacket with the other. He tossed that over a chair, impatient to pull out his phone from his pocket the moment his hand was free. A real friend, real feelings, conversation, communion—

Today, I was desperate for tater tots.

He stared at the sentence for a long moment. What the hell…?

And then, all of a sudden, life wasn't so heavy. He didn't have to take himself so seriously. Thane read the hot-pink silliness, and he started to laugh.

The rest of his clothes came off easily. Off with the tan T-shirt that clung after a day of Texas heat. Thane had to sit to unlace the combat boots, but he typed a quick line to let Ballerina know he was online. You crack me up.

And thank God for that.

He brushed his teeth. He pulled back the sheets and fell into bed, phone in one hand. He bunched his pillow up under his neck, and he realized he was smiling at his phone fondly as he typed, I'd miss you. It was crazy, but it was true.

The little cursor on his phone screen blinked. He waited, eyes drifting idly over the blue and pink words they'd already exchanged. You killed them? he'd written, followed by words like *murder. Jail.*

He was going to scare her away. She'd think he was a freak the way his mind went immediately to crime and punishment. Did normal guys—civilian guys—zing their conversations right to felony death?

She must think he was a civilian. His screen name was Different Drummer, after all, nothing that implied he was either military or in law enforcement. They weren't supposed to reveal what Ballerina called their "real, boring surface facts," things like name, address, job. During one of those marathon chat sessions where they'd spilled their guts out, they'd agreed that anonymity was part of the reason they could write to each other so freely.

He hoped the way he used so many law enforcement references didn't give away his real profession. It wasn't like he was dropping clues subconsciously. Really.

He read her words. She made him smile with *ketchup, mustard* and *salt.* He wondered if she'd kept a straight face when she wrote that, or had she giggled at her own silliness? Did she have a shy smile or a wide-open laugh?

Then she told him she had to go. He had to act like that was perfectly okay. They'd talk some other time. But before closing the app he remembered the couple downstairs—*Hi, baby, how was your day?*

Ballerina Baby was the woman who'd greeted him after a long day of work.

Looking forward to it, Baby.

A subconscious slip? He'd never called Ballerina Baby just Baby before.

She didn't reply. All his exhaustion returned with a vengeance. If Ballerina couldn't talk, what good would it do to go out to exchange nods and grunts with everyone else?

He tossed his phone onto his nightstand and rolled onto his side, ready for the sleep that would overtake him in moments. But just before it did, he thought what he could never type: You mean more to me than you should, Baby.

Chapter Two

"Friday night. Almost quitting time, Boss."

At his platoon sergeant's booming voice, Thane tossed his cell phone onto his desk, facedown. He should have known that if he decided to check his personal messages for the first time in twelve hours, someone would walk in.

Thane could have stayed on his phone, of course. This was his office, and he didn't have to stop what he was doing and stand when a noncommissioned officer, an NCO, walked in. But he didn't want his platoon sergeant to see any hot-pink words that would encourage him to start giving Thane hell about women. As a commissioned officer, Thane outranked sergeants and other noncommissioned officers, but Sergeant First Class Lloyd had been in the army more than twice as many years as Thane. A platoon sergeant was a platoon leader's right arm. The platoon didn't run well without either one of them—and no NCO let his lieutenant forget it, either.

Sergeant First Class Lloyd was older, more experienced—and married, too. In other words, he'd enjoy razzing his bachelor platoon leader about his love life. Thane wasn't going to give him a pink-fonted excuse to do it.

Thane kicked back in his government-issued desk chair and put his booted feet up on the gray desk that had probably served all the platoon leaders who'd come before him since Vietnam. Maybe even further back. The battleship-gray metal desk was old but indestructible. He liked it.

"I take it you didn't come here to tell me the CO went home." Retreat had sounded, the flag had been lowered, all the enlisted soldiers dismissed, but the lieutenants were still here because the company commander—the CO—was still here. It wasn't a written rule, but Thane was old enough to know that it wasn't wise for platoon leaders to leave before the company commander did.

"It's Friday, sir. I wouldn't still be here if the CO had left." Just as the platoon leaders didn't leave before the company commander, the platoon sergeants didn't leave before the first sergeant did. Since the first sergeant didn't leave before the company commander did, here they all were, waiting for Friday night to begin.

Thane watched his platoon sergeant head for the empty desk next to his own. Was the man going to take a seat and settle in for a chat? It wasn't like him. Sergeant First Class Lloyd was a man of few words.

"Do you have any big plans for the weekend, sir?" asked the noncommissioned officer of few words.

"Just the usual."

"Kicking ass and taking names?"

"Not tonight. Lieutenant Salvatore has duty."

The man started pulling out desk drawers, then slamming them shut. "Whiskey and women then, sir?"

"Also not happening tonight." Thane leaned back a little more in his chair and tucked his hands behind his head. "Sleep. Nothing but sweet sleep."

His platoon sergeant spared him a quick glance. "You pulled another thirty-six hours, sir?"

An affirmative grunt was enough of an answer.

Without further comment, Sergeant First Class Lloyd sat in the desk chair and started testing its tilt and the height of its armrests.

"What are you doing?" Thane finally asked. "You planning on buying that chair after this test ride?"

"No, sir. Just seeing if I should permanently borrow it before the new platoon leader arrives."

Thane sat up, boots hitting the floor. "Don't get my hopes up, Sergeant First Class. Is there a new platoon leader coming in?"

"Yes, sir. In-processing on post."

"About damn time." Thane didn't like the look on the

sergeant's face, though. "Let's hear it. I can tell you got more intel."

"Brand-new second lieutenant, fresh out of Leonard Wood."

Fort Leonard Wood, Missouri, was the home of the Military Police Corps. All new second lieutenants had to go through the four months of BOLC, Basic Officer Leadership Course, there. If that was all his platoon sergeant had on the new guy, it hardly counted as intel.

Thane leaned back and laced his fingers behind his head once more. "It's that time of year. The college boys all graduate in May and complete BOLC in the fall. It would be too much to hope for to get someone with experience. It's butter bar season."

The term *butter bar* referred to the yellow color of the single bar that denoted the rank of second lieutenant. As a first lieutenant, Thane's rank insignia was a black bar on the camouflaged ACUs he wore almost every day, or a silver bar on the dress uniform.

"Sergeant First Class Ernesto has broken in his fair share of lieutenants," Thane said. "I'm sure he'll handle this one. I just want someone to throw into the duty officer rotation. A butter bar will work."

Sergeant First Class Ernesto was the platoon sergeant for fourth platoon. He'd been running fourth platoon without a platoon leader for three months, attending all the first sergeant's meetings for NCOs and then the commander's meetings for the platoon leaders, as well. Thane would bet money that fourth platoon's sergeant felt the same way he did. Even a wet-behind-the-ears butter bar would be better than nothing.

"Well, sir, you'll get to update that duty roster soon enough. The new LT already had one ride-along. A couple more ride-alongs this weekend, and you can add that name to your schedule."

"Do you have a name yet?"

"Second Lieutenant Michaels. I'll be right back." Lloyd rolled the office chair out the door. Each office in the head-quarters building held two desks. While fourth platoon had no lieutenant, Lloyd had been using the desk next to Ernesto, two NCOs doing their NCO thing, but the new platoon leader would be in Ernesto's office now. Thane would have to get used to having his own platoon sergeant sharing this room again.

He picked up his cell phone and unlocked the screen. Pink words awaited him. Something came up, and I won't be able to be by the phone tonight. There goes our Star Trek marathon. I'm sorry. The best-laid plans of mice and men...

They'd planned to write each other while watching the same channel tonight—so he knew Ballerina Baby lived in the United States somewhere and got the sci-fi channel on cable—but it looked like his evening was suddenly free. And more boring. The disappointment was sharp, but he had to play it cool. He wasn't her boyfriend. He couldn't demand to know why she was changing her plans, and he shouldn't demand it. If Ballerina said she couldn't make it, he believed her. Thane frowned. He also wasn't sure who'd said the mice and men line.

Shakespeare? That was right nine times out of ten.

Gotcha. Robbie Burns. You're not a fan of Scottish poetry?

Damn. She'd gotten him last week with Burns, raving about how she loved her new sofa that was the color of a red, red rose. No, but I'm a fan of Star Trek and I'm a fan of you. Now I only get one of those two things tonight.

His platoon sergeant came back in, pushing a chair with squeaky wheels ahead of himself. Thane turned his phone screen off. With all the pink and blue letters, it practically looked like a baby announcement. Lloyd would have a field day with that.

Thane stood up. "I'll help you move the rest of your stuff. You prefer the squeaky wheels, huh?"

"No, sir. That's why I just upgraded. I'm going to leave this chair here."

"You're not moving back in?"

Lloyd had that grin on his face again, the one Thane didn't trust. "Well, sir, maybe an experienced lieutenant like yourself ought to show the new lieutenant the ropes. Maybe we should keep one office NCOs, one office lieutenants."

"No. No way. You're not sticking me with some fresh college kid. He's Ernesto's problem to deal with, not mine. That's what a platoon sergeant is for, to keep the rookie LT out of trouble."

Lloyd only grinned wider. "It's not my idea. Seems like the CO thinks you'd be the best man for the job. He told the first sergeant who he wants in each office. He wants you to babysit Lieutenant Michaels. I mean, train Lieutenant Michaels."

Thane cursed and rubbed his hand over his jaw and its five o'clock shadow, suddenly feeling each one of the thirty-six hours he'd been working. He'd wanted a fourth platoon leader to come in to lighten his work routine, but he hadn't wanted that new platoon leader to impact his daily routine this much. "That explains the grin on your face. I don't suppose there's any chance this lieutenant is OCS?"

OCS stood for Officer Candidate School. It was the quickest way for an enlisted soldier who already had a college degree to become an officer. Thane had only had a high school diploma when he'd enlisted, so he'd applied for an ROTC scholarship. After he'd served two years as an enlisted man, the army had changed his rank from corporal to ROTC cadet and sent him to four years of college on the army's dime. His prior two years as an infantry grunt made him a little older than most first lieutenants. He thought it made him a little wiser as well, since most ROTC grads were entering the army for the first time. If this butter bar was coming to them from OCS instead of ROTC, then he'd have some prior service, and he wouldn't be as much of a rookie. But Lloyd was still smiling. Not good.

"No, sir. Not OCS. Not ROTC, either. The word is that Lieutenant Michaels is fresh out of West Point."

"Are you kidding me?" The third way to become an officer was by attending the United States Military Academy at West Point, one of the country's oldest and most elite schools. *Elite* meant there weren't very many West Pointers in the army in general. Thane had worked with several, of course, and he couldn't honestly say he'd ever had a problem with a West Point graduate, but anything elite was automatically met with suspicion by everyone else, including him.

"Monday morning, sir, you get to share all your special secret lieutenant-y wisdom with a brand-new West Pointer. I'll be over in Ernesto's office if you need me."

"You're so helpful."

"You've been up since yesterday morning, sir. The CO hasn't. You should go home now." But as Lloyd left the office, he stopped and turned around. "Oh, and one more thing. Your new butter bar West Pointer office buddy? Word is that Lieutenant Michaels is a girl. See you Monday, Boss."

I wish I could sleep another four hours, but I'm burning too much daylight as is.

Thane glanced at the pink words as he poured raw scrambled eggs into a cast-iron skillet. Ballerina was going to have to dig deeper than that if she was going to stump him today. He'd slept until noon. The duty schedule had finally coincided with the right days on the calendar, and Thane had a whopping forty-eight hours off. He'd left the office Friday evening and didn't have to be anywhere until he took over at the police station on Sunday evening.

He typed on his phone with one finger while he kept his

Saturday morning eggs moving around with the spatula in his other hand. John Wayne. (Too easy. Really.) Why so tired?

Late night.

His flash of jealousy wasn't easy to laugh off. A single woman out late on a Friday night? Thane knew, somehow, that Ballerina would have no shortage of interested men around her. He had no idea what she looked like, but she was so full of life, so fun and quirky, men must find her as attractive in real life as he found her online. She must laugh and smile a lot with her real friends; there was nothing more attractive. Or maybe she was shy, making intelligent wise-cracks under her breath only to the one friend standing next to her. Also attractive.

This old app had no photo features. It didn't matter what she looked like, anyway. She was attractive to him in a way that went beyond blonde, brunette or redhead. Not only did it not matter, it would never matter. Other men would compete to get her smiles and hugs. He had no chance of being one of those men, the one who would pursue her until he was her favorite out of them all, until he was the only man she wanted to be with.

He should be satisfied that he was the man who got her thoughts and words, at least for now. When she found someone to love, he wouldn't even have that. Thane grabbed a fork and started eating from the skillet, standing up. Jealousy over a pen pal was stupid and he knew it. But...

She hadn't been able to chat with him last night, because she'd gone out somewhere.

He stabbed the eggs a little viciously. All right, so Ballerina had a life. He could keep this in perspective. She'd said something last night about working off that bag of tater tots she'd eaten. Maybe she'd had a rehearsal or even a performance. If she wasn't a ballerina, he still suspected she was involved with dance, maybe a dance instructor, or a choreographer. Like him, she often mentioned going to work out or being tired from a vaguely described workout.

He shoveled in more eggs and began to type. Out late for work or play?

There was a bit of a pause before she answered. Is this a trick question to see if I'll give you a clue about what I do for a living? Do I work at night?

Busted. Of course it was.

Of course not. How about this—did you enjoy your late night or were you gutting it out?

I loved it. I'm a natural night owl. I wish more of the world was. Even as a little kid, I hated going to bed for school. Kindergarten is misery for night owlets. Owlings. Whatever the term is. Why couldn't school have been from 8pm to 2am, instead of 8am to 2pm?

He put down the fork to type with two thumbs. You should've been a vampire. Do they have school-aged vampires? A kindergarten full of little ankle biters—literally, biters—who want school to start at 8 at night.

That doesn't seem right, she answered. I think you have to be a grown-up and choose to become a vampire. I don't think I would, though. I feel isolated enough already. If I became a vampire, I'd be so sad, watching everyone I know going to bed and knowing by the time they woke up, I'd be done for the day. I'll just have to stay a human night owl. (Is that an oxymoron? A human owl?) I don't have many night owl friends, though. In fact, you're the only one I can chat with at 3 in the morning. And because I know how to follow the ground rules, I'm not going to ask why you're sometimes awake at 3.

I'm a vampire.

Ha ha. I'm just glad that you're a night owl, too. You really are the perfect pen pal for me.

Thane finished his eggs and left the iron skillet to cool. At least one woman out there thought he was perfect because of his crazy military schedule, not despite it. His last girlfriend, a civilian he still ran into too often in the small world of an army town, had pouted every night and weekend that he had to work. Pouting wasn't as cute as it sounded.

Do you know the longest amount of time I've gone without talking to you? Ten days. And by talking, I mean writing to you in hot-pink letters, of course. Stupid app. It's so cliché, pink ink for girls and blue ink for boys.

I know. I'm so used to it now, I get startled when I type anywhere else and the words are black instead of blue.

I love this app, though, because it made us pen pals. I enjoy talking with you as much as with any friend I've ever had.

Thane smiled down at the phone screen. After a long pause, more pink appeared.

Do you think that's normal?

He stopped smiling. The answer, of course, was no. It wasn't normal. He took the phone out to his balcony, all four feet by two feet of concrete perch, three stories above the earth, and looked down to the complex's central swimming pool. Management had posted signs by the mailboxes that there would be a party today with free food. That party had started without him.

He didn't care. There was no one down there he'd rather be talking with. If it isn't normal, then we're both abnormal. It's easy to talk to you.

Agreed. Real people are hard.

I'm real, he wanted to write. But he didn't.
Do you have a close friend in real life? she asked.

Define friend.

I think that means no. If you had a close friend, you'd just say yes. You wouldn't ask me what a close friend is.

She had him there.

But I think you're normal...for a blue ink person. I read somewhere that the majority of married women will say their female friends are their best friends, when asked. But the majority of men will say their wife is their best friend. I remember that because I thought it was sad that there are apparently a lot of husbands out there who think their wife is their best friend, but she prefers a female buddy. Are you really best friends with someone if that person doesn't think you are their best friend, too? It's too much like unrequited love.

Who was his closest friend? His platoon sergeant came to mind immediately. They worked together every day, aiming for the same goals. They relied on one another. But Sergeant First Class Lloyd was not someone who would catch a famous quote in conversation—or who would laugh about it if he did. Heck, the platoon sergeant couldn't even call Thane by his first name. Thane was addressed as Lieutenant Carter or Sir. Sometimes LT, the abbreviation of lieutenant, or, if they were being really casual, Boss. That was it.

His company commander was another good man. More than a boss in the civilian sense of the word, but not a buddy. They shared some laughs, they were on the same page when it came to training and discipline, and they'd spent one Sun-

day in the field huddled over the same radio to get the play
off scores, because they cheered for the same NFL team
But the company commander was always the commander
with all the legal authority and responsibility that the posi
tion entailed. Thane was always Lieutenant Carter, no mat
ter how many whiskeys they'd downed during officer-only
dining-in events in the brigade.

Thane was pretty sure Ballerina Baby would expect him
to call a close friend by his first name, at a minimum.

The only people at work who didn't call him Lieutenant
Carter were the other two platoon leaders. They were good
guys. One was married, one was not. The married guy's wife
was named... Cecilia? Serena? Something with an *s* sound.
If you couldn't name a friend's wife, he probably wouldn'
qualify as a close friend in Ballerina's book. The other pla
toon leader was from Phoenix. Thane felt like he should ge
points for knowing that...okay, not a close friend. A friend
though. More than an acquaintance.

Laughter from the pool floated up to his balcony. Maybe
he ought to care more that he didn't have a friend at his own
apartment complex.

He tried to put the ball back in Ballerina's court. Do you
have a real friend in real life?

Then he waited. She'd probably say yes. Jealousy reared
its ugly green head again, and in that moment, he realized
how selfish that was. His life didn't allow him to make
friends in a normal way. Military rules didn't allow him to
date any woman who interested him. Military schedules were
demanding. Did he wish the same for Ballerina Baby? Just
because he felt isolated, just because he felt lonely among
the very same people whom he would willingly fight beside, that was no reason for him to wish the same for her.
He wanted her to have it better.

Her reply was a question. You're real, aren't you, Drummer?

Poor Ballerina. She was the same as he, sharing all her

emotions with a stranger through an app. It filled a need, for certain, but even she didn't call him by his first name. No one called him by name.

Whose fault was that?

Thane looked at the pool party with new eyes. If he wanted someone in real life who would call him by name, then he should do something about it. He could start by putting on his board shorts and flip-flops, going down there and telling people his real name. "Hello, I'm Thane." And that would be followed by...

What? Awkward small talk. He and Ballerina had moved past that quickly, months ago. He wasn't the kind of guy who told jokes, but Ballerina answered his attempts at humor with her little pink *Ha*. That wouldn't be happening in the group down there, people who were laughing between the barbecue grill and the keg of beer.

Thane Carter in apartment 601 left his balcony and shut the door against the Texas heat and the party noise.

I'm real, Baby, and I'm here for you.

Chloe Michaels in apartment 401 wriggled into a sitting position on the floor of her new living room, sitting up with her back against a moving box. She never took her eyes off her laptop screen.

I'm real, Baby, and I'm here for you.

She slid right down to the carpet again. Jeez. The most romantic words she ever heard weren't spoken, but typed.

Drummer was the perfect man, and she was so glad to have him in her life. Normal or abnormal, she couldn't help but spin fantasies about a man who was so open with her. Her latest was that he might be a billionaire, for example, so determined to find out who she was and where she lived that he'd buy the company that ran this pen pal app. Then he'd find her when she wasn't expecting it. He'd stride up to her and say, "Hello, I'm Drummer. I wanted to meet you, touch you, kiss you and take you away from all this."

Of course, even a billionaire couldn't tell the US Army they didn't own her for the next five years. She would stay a lieutenant no matter whom she met and fell in love with. Frankly, she wouldn't want to go anywhere. She'd been sworn into the army as a new cadet just two weeks after she'd graduated from high school, and she'd been training ever since to be an officer. She wanted to do what she'd been trained to do.

She looked up from her laptop. Through her sliding glass door, past the edge of her little concrete balcony, she could see the swimming pool in the center of the complex. It was crowded. There'd been a flyer posted by the mailboxes about free burgers at the pool today. It looked like a full-on party to her.

This was where she lived now, and even if a billionaire named Different Drummer went to extremes to find her and then declared his undying love for her, she would not only stay a lieutenant, she would continue to be stationed right here in Texas. For years.

She ought to make friends here.

Drummer's icon flashed, indicating he was typing. Her heart did a little happy flip. They could type back and forth like this for an hour or two or more. They'd done just that many times.

Ok, Miss John Wayne, you said you were burning daylight. Big plans?

Chloe looked out to the pool. She had no doubt she was typing to a real person, but he wasn't a billionaire and he couldn't come sweep her off her feet.

I've been invited to a party. I want to take a nap, but I think I should go.

Why?

We just established that we don't have any close friends except each other. I love

Chloe stopped typing. She deleted the word *love*. They'd agreed that they were either normal or abnormal together. She didn't want to cross that line from abnormal to freaky-girl-with-fantasies. She typed *like*.

I like our long chats. I would miss you, too, if we couldn't write one another. But it wouldn't hurt to have friends around here. I might need a ride to the airport, you know, or need to call someone to jump-start my car battery. I know you'd reach through the clutter of all these pink and blue letters to lend a hand if you could, but since you can't, I ought to go to this party just to meet the people in my neighborhood. Could be a fireman or a postman in my neighborhood, you know? Right here on my very own street.

She hit Send. Good grief, she felt like she was cheating on the man, or at the very least suggesting to a boyfriend that they start seeing other people. She'd paraphrased what she could remember from an old song from Sesame Street, as if sounding like a cute child would soften her words. *Abnormal* was a mild term for her.

You should go. You'll make friends fast, I know it.

Oh. Chloe blinked at her screen in surprise. He wanted her to sign off and go to the party. What had she expected? That he would beg her to stay by her computer and talk to him and only him this weekend? He hadn't caught the reference to the children's show, either. She felt lonelier than ever. She couldn't exactly tell Drummer that she'd rather type to him than meet real people, even though it was true.

She wrote a different truth. I appreciate your vote of confidence in my ability to make friends, but I don't go to many parties. I doubt I'll make friends fast. I'm not really a "life of the party" kind of girl.

That was an understatement. While it seemed everyone else was pulling keggers at their civilian colleges, alcohol was forbidden in the barracks at West Point, and cadets weren't free to come and go as they pleased on or off post. Cadets who were caught breaking those rules faced serious punishment, even expulsion. Ergo, her party experience was about four years behind the average twenty-two-year-old's.

Drummer's answer was kind. Anyone who quotes Sesame Street is sure to make friends. How could anyone not like a person like you?

She felt a pang in her chest. He'd gotten it. He got *her.* If only…

I wish I knew you'd be there. It would be so much easier to put myself out there and say hello to strangers if I knew, at some point as I worked my way through the room, I'd eventually end up next to you. I'd be so glad to see your friendly face, and we'd kind of huddle together in a corner and ignore everyone as we updated each other on who was who at the party. I'd tell you not to leave me alone with the guy who just spent ten minutes lecturing me on the virtues of colon cleanses, and you'd say "What? That wasn't the start of a beautiful friendship?"

One swift, blue word: Casablanca.

LOL. Yes, and we'd spend the rest of the party hanging out

together and talking only to each other, nonstop, and I'd be so glad I came.

Chloe looked at her little pink scenario fondly. A little sadly. This was an even better fantasy than the silly billionaire one, but neither one could come true.

If that's what you want, Ballerina, then let's do that. There's an event I could go to today, too. We'll find each other afterward, and tell each other who was who at our respective outings. I want you to have a friend to call if your car battery dies. I could use one, too, for that ride to the airport. Let's do this together. Deal?

Chloe looked at the friendly blue words, happiness and sadness warring within her. He was the perfect guy and he'd come up with a perfect solution, but the bottom line was that they both needed to find someone perfect outside of this app.

If she went out, he'd go out. So, for his sake as well as her own, she started looking around her apartment for the box most likely to be hiding her bathing suit.

It's a deal. Talk to you later.

Looking forward to it, Baby.

Chapter Three

Life was better than she'd expected it to be.

The realization hit Chloe as she stood on her third-story balcony, performing a recon on the party down below. The Central Texas landscape was brown and sparse when she looked in between the identical buildings toward the horizon, but if she looked down, she saw a sparkling blue swimming pool. It was fall, but this was Texas, and there was plenty of warmth and sun to be had. Maybe Central Texas was more desert than tropical, but the whole apartment complex felt like a resort hotel to her.

Life had been pretty Spartan for the past four years. Room assignments at West Point had changed every semester; she'd had no choice but to move from one end of the same barracks hallway to the other, again and again and again. She'd always had a roommate, and they'd always slept in their assigned twin beds in alphabetical order. When she roomed with Schweitzer, Chloe Michaels slept on the left side of the room, because Michaels outranked Schweitzer alphabetically. When she roomed with Chavez, she slept on the right, but always, no matter which semester and no matter what her rank, she slept on a twin bed made up with a gray wool blanket that was stretched taut and tucked tightly into hospital corners, every single day for four years.

After graduation, the Basic Officer Leadership Course had housed her in the BOQ, the Bachelor Officer Quarters, at Fort Leonard Wood. The mini-apartment had seemed like a luxury despite being furnished in institutional army style with a vinyl couch and a chunky, square coffee table that had survived a whole lot of boots resting on it. Once more, she'd had an assigned roommate, but they'd had an actual kitchen. No more eating whatever was served in the mess hall three times a day. Even better, she'd had a bedroom with only one twin bed in it and a door that closed for privacy. That was a real luxury.

But now…

Chloe surveyed her new world. The complex had been built fairly recently, so everything was current, from the fresh paint on the buildings to the fresh carpet in her apartment. It wasn't a long drive to post, and while there were cheaper places to live, this apartment was still in her budget. She didn't need a roommate to split costs. She had the whole place to herself.

But the biggest luxury of all was this: the army hadn't told her to live here. She could live anywhere she wanted to, as long as she showed up for duty. She'd visited five different apartment complexes. She'd chosen this place, Two Rivers Apartments. That was more than a luxury. That was freedom.

How strange—how intoxicating—to realize she'd never have to stand at attention during a room inspection again. She'd crossed a finish line in a race she'd been running since the day she'd graduated from high school. This was it. This was the view from the winner's circle, a blue pool that she could swim in if she wanted to, or ignore altogether. Freedom.

She went inside, making a beeline for her laptop, an automatic reflex to share her joy with Drummer, before she remembered that he wasn't online. He was at an event. She was supposed to go to a pool party and make a friend, someone who was not him. Someone who was not whom she really wanted to be talking to. Her pleasure dimmed a little bit, but she was going to keep her word and go, and then she was going to cozy up with Drummer later and tell him all about it.

She closed her laptop and headed down the stairs. The flip-flops that left her toes bare and the sundress that left her shoulders bare felt exotic. Her hair swished over her shoulders with each step and tickled her cheek. As a cadet, she'd only had an hour or two each night before taps when, if she stayed in her barracks room to study, she could let her hair down. At BOLC, she'd been able to wear it down when she was in civilian clothes, which had been most weekends. Now, she intended to pin it up only when she was at work. Luxury. Freedom. Control over her own hair.

There was music coming from the pool. She could smell burgers on the grill. Those were things she'd be able to put into words when she wrote to Drummer tonight. But she didn't know how to describe the change in her life, this pay-off for years of hard work, for years of voluntarily subjecting herself to strict rules and a demanding regimen, all with the hope that someday, she would be done and it would all have been worth it.

Someday was today.

Today is the first day of the rest of my life. That quote would do, but she didn't know who'd said it or in which book or movie.

I'm saying it.

Yes, she was. She'd arrived at the party—figuratively and literally. Chloe opened the gate to walk onto the white concrete pool decking. Life was good and it was only going to get better.

And that was when she saw…him.

Their eyes met across a crowded pool deck.

Thane had never seen her before. He would have remembered if she'd gotten out of a car in the parking lot or checked her mail in the stairwell. Her hair was long but not too long. Brown but not very dark, almost blond in the sunlight. She was tall-ish. And since they were staring at each other a moment too long, he could tell from this side of the pool that her eyes were as dark as his were light. She'd come through that gate smiling, like she was eager to be here, and that smile never dimmed as their gazes met and held.

He liked the way she looked.

Then the moment was over because she turned away to

claim a chair, kicking off her flip-flops underneath it. She shook off a small case that dangled from her wrist by a strap and let it drop on the seat of the chair. It looked like a wallet. Thane's law enforcement training automatically calculated the odds for a theft. She shouldn't leave it sitting on a chair in plain view, even though this was hardly a high-crime area.

The apartment rent was just a little more than his monthly military housing allowance, an amount that increased as a soldier's rank increased. Everyone here could afford about the same apartment, which meant everyone here was about the same rank, first or second lieutenants, a few bachelor captains, and a handful of mid-career sergeants whose allowances were equal to a new lieutenant's. Not a hotbed of thieves, in Thane's professional police opinion, but still, she shouldn't leave a wallet out in plain sight like that.

She kept her back to him as she pulled off her sundress over her head. She wore a bikini underneath, but it was the sport kind like the female competitors wore on TV in beach volleyball or Ironman competitions. The suit suited her, so to speak. She wasn't just slender, she was toned, the muscles in her arms and legs tight—nicely firm backside, too. He fully appreciated the sight of a physically fit woman baring an acre of smooth skin to the sun. Whoever had come up with the idea for a pool party was a genius.

She rolled her wallet up in the dress and tucked it in with her shoes underneath the chair, out of sight. Beauty, athleticism, common sense—he'd definitely never seen her around here before. Which meant the odds were that she was someone's guest, which sucked, because the apartment residents were mostly male, so the odds were that she was here as some other man's guest.

Or maybe not. She peeked to see if he was still there, a millisecond of a glance, before she pretended she wasn't aware of him and studiously looked toward the barbecue crowd instead. The smile still lingered on her lips.

I'm still here, beautiful. It's okay to be interested in me. I'm interested in you.

Thane tore his eyes away from that smile to look where she was looking. None of the men around the grill seemed to be searching for his girlfriend. *Be single, be single. This could be the start of a beautiful friendship.*

Casablanca—in a flash, Thane thought of Ballerina and felt…guilty. Like he was cheating on her, which was ridiculous. They'd agreed they needed real-life friends and were both going out today to try to meet some. Instead, in had walked this beautiful woman, and his mind had chucked the friend quest far away and pulled the idea of a girlfriend close. That was fine, though. There was no reason in the world why he couldn't find a real-life girlfriend. After all, a girlfriend could jump-start a car or give him a lift to the airport and do all those things a pen pal couldn't do.

The woman—the very real woman—slid her hand under her hair and lifted it from the back of her neck for a moment. Then she let it go again, all that feminine hair falling over all that bare skin.

Thane looked away and took a deeper breath, a little extra oxygen to keep his thoughts from going haywire. But there was no doubt his thoughts were heading toward a whole new category of things that a pen pal couldn't do.

"How about those Cowboys?"

One of the mailbox guys called the question to him while working the tap of a keg, filling a red Solo cup with beer. He held up one that was already full and nodded toward Thane with that look that said, *Do you want one?*

Thane took it from him with a nod of thanks. "I think the Cowboys will take the Packers tomorrow. You back from a deployment?"

"Yeah." His neighbor shrugged.

"Thought so," Thane answered. "Hadn't seen you around in a while."

His neighbor lifted his now-full beer in a bit of a toast,

then sauntered away from the keg as Thane took a step in the other direction.

That was it, the complete guy conversation. Same as always.

It reminded Thane why he was here. He headed around the edge of the pool, walking with a purpose to get to the other side. He wanted someone to call him by his first name, and he knew exactly which person he wanted that to be.

"Chloe!"

And…damn it. There was the man she must have been looking for. Thane slowed his steps and took in the scene. The beautiful woman, Chloe, hugged the shirtless man who'd just run up to her with all the eagerness of a golden retriever.

Okay, so Thane wasn't feeling too kind. The man slobbering for her attention was probably just a couple of years younger than Thane, and probably an officer, too. But that man had something Thane didn't. He apparently had the affection of one woman named Chloe, whose smile for him was open, unrestrained. Dazzling.

Thane walked around the edge of the pool to her side. He was at the farthest corner from her, but even from this distance, that smile was everything. Some guys were breast men and some were into legs, and while Thane was all in favor of all of that, it was Chloe's smile that really knocked his socks off. It was happiness. Who could resist happiness?

Apparently not the men around this pool. Two more men left the grill and hugged Chloe. She was surrounded. The guys all looked the same. Everyone had a military haircut, everyone was physically fit, no one was younger than twenty-one and no one had reached thirty yet. Only Chloe was special. Thane couldn't take his eyes off her.

He didn't think she was in the military. She had the fitness thing going on, but there was something about her bearing…

She was too relaxed. In the eight years since he'd first enlisted, he'd come to realize that military life tended to make soldiers feel like they were stealing moments of fun or relaxation between deployments or missions or shifts, which was how he felt because it was indeed what he was doing. This woman looked like she had time, like she was where she wanted to be and enjoying it.

Maybe she was a local. She could be a yoga instructor, all smooth muscle and Zen contentment, the polar opposite of him and his career.

The guys around her talked over one another, laughing and gesturing. Chloe was laughing with them, but this didn't look like a boyfriend introducing his girlfriend to his pals. This looked like a reunion of people who were surprised to find each other here. Long-lost college buddies, maybe. That kind of thing happened in an army town all the time. Paths crossed unexpectedly with so many people coming and going as assignments began and ended.

She glanced his way and did a subtle double take when she saw that he was walking directly toward her. She didn't look away. Neither did he.

Another man came running up behind her, full speed. She started to turn with an elbow raised in a defensive move but the man plowed into her, wrapped his arms around her in a bear hug and let his momentum carry them off the edge of the pool to plunge into the water.

Idiot.

Thane didn't know a woman alive who appreciated getting thrown into a pool without warning. That fabulous smile of hers was going to be gone.

They popped up a couple of feet apart.

"Idiot," Chloe said.

Exactly.

But then Chloe broke into laughter. "You are so, so lucky you still have all your teeth, Keith. I was about to clock you with my elbow when I realized it was you. You better be grateful I've got ninja-like mastery of my ninja-like reflexes." They exchanged trash-talking banter until Chloe hoisted herself out of the pool.

Okay, she didn't sound like a Zen yogini. She'd gotten in some good zingers, though. Now she sat on the edge, her hair a waterfall down her back, her feet still in the pool. "I don't suppose any of you guys brought a towel? I don't have one. I wasn't planning on going in."

"Me, neither," said one of the dry guys. "Sorry."

"The sun's out," said another dry guy. "You'll be fine."

"Hey, the keg's been tapped." The tackling guy hauled himself out of the pool and headed over to the keg, dripping wet.

College buddies, for sure. If any one of them wanted to try to become more, he'd best get his act together. Thane wasn't going to hang back and wait for the pack of golden retrievers to grow up and man up.

Thane detoured a few steps to the chair where he'd thrown his things earlier and snagged his oversize towel with one hand. Then he walked up to the pool's edge and crouched down beside Chloe. "I've got an untouched beer here and a clean towel. You're welcome to one or the other or both."

"I'll take the towel, please."

They were strangers, so her smile for him was polite, pleasant, still beautiful. Thane set down the beer so he could shake out the towel and let it fall around her shoulders, keeping the action quick and casual. "There you go."

"Thanks."

He picked up the beer and sat next to her, putting his feet in the water, too.

She beat him to the introductions, holding out her wet hand for a shake. "And hi, by the way. My name is Chloe."

"My name is Thane. I wanted to meet you."

They smiled at one another.

This feels like the start of a beautiful friendship.

Chapter Four

They'd arrived late to the party, so the burgers were all gone.

Thane didn't care. Nothing could ruin this day. He'd met a girl, and now the sun was warmer, the trees were greener, the food smelled better. He could keep talking to her forever. He wanted to learn more about her, where she came from, how she felt about everything, where she was going. He wanted to keep looking at her beautiful face. There would be a first date, a first kiss. He couldn't wait for time to speed toward that moment; he was enjoying every second right now and didn't want this afternoon to end.

"It looks like our choice is hot dogs or hot dogs," she said to him. To the complex's maintenance man who was manning the grill, she said, "I'd like a hot dog, please."

Thane got two for himself and they headed over to the condiment table, where, unfortunately, two of the four golden retrievers were hovering. Chloe made the introductions. Marcus shook his hand. Bill had a beer in one hand and a plate in the other, so he did the lift of the chin. Of course.

"We went to school together," Chloe offered. Her hair was still wet but not dripping. She'd tied Thane's towel around herself, high under her arms. It made her look like she'd just stepped out of a shower. It was a very, very good look.

Judging from the way their gazes kept straying to the knot in the towel that rested just above her breasts, Bill and Marcus thought so, too. Bill turned away pretty quickly to set down his beer and pick up the mustard for his hot dog. If he cared more about mustard than hanging on to Chloe's every word, then he probably had something else going on with a different woman.

"Hey, are you still serious with that girl from Mount Saint Mary's?" Chloe asked Bill.

Thane wondered if she'd read his mind. Nah—Chloe

wasn't vain enough to assume every single man ought to be interested in her. Except every single man around here was—just not Bill.

Chloe pointed to Bill's plate. "You only put mustard on your hot dog. That reminded me about her."

"Mustard made you think of Susie?" Bill asked.

"Don't you remember the hot dog test? Mustard means a man wants to settle down."

"Oh, that dorky thing. I remember." He looked at his hot dog and started to laugh. "You aren't going to believe this, but Susie and I got engaged when I finished Airborne School."

The other dude dropped the mustard like it had burned him. "Which topping was for the good-looking men who like to show women a good time?"

"Marcus the man-whore," Bill muttered under his breath.

"I can't tell you," Chloe said. "That would invalidate the whole hot dog test."

Thane listened with one ear as he covered one hot dog with relish. Across the pool deck, he spotted one little table left in the shade. He'd ask Chloe if she wanted to go over there. Hopefully, the pack wouldn't follow. They weren't bad guys; they just weren't a beautiful woman wrapped in his towel, which was the only person Thane cared to talk to. He picked up the ketchup bottle and squeezed a hearty red line over the relish dog.

"The opposite of married is bachelor, which is what I am," Marcus said. "Suave and devastating bachelor. The opposite of mustard is ketchup, so it must be ketchup."

"That's right," Chloe said, and then a little silence followed as everyone looked at Thane.

He held the ketchup bottle in the air a second longer, then set it down.

"So, you're a playboy bachelor?" Chloe asked with a tilt of her head and a teasing voice.

He looked her in the eye as he silently picked up the mustard and squeezed that on his second hot dog.

Her friends loved it. Marcus nudged her with his arm. "So, what's that mean, Chloe?"

"I'm not done yet." Thane picked up a forkful of sauerkraut and plopped that on the mustard dog. The men hammed it up, their *whoa* and *watch out* sounding like they were watching a cage match.

Chloe didn't say a word. She just looked at him with that tilt of her head and a raised eyebrow, a smile threatening to break through her mock-serious expression.

Thane held up his plate. One dog with ketchup and relish, one dog with mustard and sauerkraut. That was genuinely how he liked them, so he raised an eyebrow, too. "Well? What does this mean?"

"It means," she said, her smile breaking through as her voice dropped into a quiet purr, "that you are a very interesting man."

"Watch out, everybody." Bill held up his beer and plate and took a step back. "Get out of Chloe's way."

Thane kept his focus on Chloe. "Let's see how you dress your hot dog."

"Can't do that." She held up her plate with her still-plain hot dog. "You see, I prefer mine…naked."

Marcus took a step back. "That's it, I'm outta here. Retreat."

Thane let Chloe lead the way to the little iron-lattice patio table in the shade. When they'd been sitting on the edge of the pool, feet swishing the water and accidentally touching now and then, she'd asked most of the questions. He'd lived at Two Rivers since it opened two years ago, he was from South Carolina, yeah, still a touch of the accent, and no, he hadn't been home since last Thanksgiving, a little less than a year now. It was a fifteen-, sixteen-hour drive so you really needed to fly and flying sucked lately, and yes, Austin was less than an hour's drive from here. Great city.

It was his turn. "Do you live here at Two Rivers or did your friends invite you over?"

"I live here."

"You must have just moved in."

"One whole week ago. What made you guess that?"

Thane polished off his first hot dog. "There's no way I wouldn't have noticed you already if you'd been living here for more than a week."

She went a little still at that. He hadn't said it like a cheesy pick-up line. He'd stated it as the fact that it was. Maybe that had been too direct. Maybe he was too accustomed to speaking bluntly during military operations. It was the truth, though, and she seemed like the kind of person who could handle a straightforward comment. She dealt with a pack of lieutenants like they were her brothers, when he suspected they were really angling for more. Surely, she could handle him.

"You're just flattering me now." She popped the last bite of her naked hot dog into her mouth. "I like it."

Yep. She could handle him.

"You're in the army, aren't you?" he guessed.

She nodded her head as she chewed, but for the first time, her expression dimmed a little. She was watching him closely for his reaction.

Were there men out there dumb enough to pass up a chance to spend time with her because she was in the military? Yeah, he knew a few guys like that. Old-school chauvinists. Insecure cavemen. Their loss.

She swallowed her last bite. "Is that a bad thing?"

"I hope not, since I'm in the army, too." He winked at her. She laughed.

She was too young to be one of the NCOs who lived here, but just to be safe, he pointed to the center of his chest, where his rank would be if he wore ACUs. "First lieutenant."

She tapped the knot of the towel. "Second lieutenant." *Perfect.*

Thane pushed his plate out of the way and leaned forward, resting his forearms on the table. "It's not a bad thing that we're both in the service. It just makes it a little more challenging to coordinate our schedules if we wanted to do something like go to a movie. I'm willing to try it, though, if you'd like to go see a movie." Maybe he was holding his breath, maybe he was praying she wouldn't turn him down.

She leaned forward, too, and put her arms on the table. "That sounds like fun. Since you've been here a few years, you can show me which theaters are the nicest."

"I'll take you to the best one." He meant it. The pickings were generally slim in army towns, but Fort Hood was the largest post in America, so Killeen had become a good-sized city with it. Dinner, movie, drinks—he'd take her to only the best places. He had the crazy thought that he'd be doing those places a favor, letting them be graced by a woman who radiated such happiness. Dinner and a movie in Killeen would be just the start. He'd love to take her into Austin.

"What made you guess that I was in the army?" she asked. "I thought I was being a pretty normal civilian. I haven't been speaking in acronyms, have I?"

He chuckled and leaned back in his chair. "You asked how far it was to Austin, so you're obviously new to the area. The main reason new people pour into Killeen is because the army sent them here." He nodded toward the apartment buildings. "And the main reason people live here is because it's conveniently priced for a junior officer's housing allowance."

She chuckled, too, and leaned back in her chair.

This couldn't be going better. God, I'm glad I came.

"I thought my friends gave it away with their regulation haircuts. I didn't even know they were going to be stationed at Hood. I just ran into Keith at the PX yesterday, so I knew he was at Hood, but I didn't know he lived here in Two Rivers. Keith's the one who went swimming."

"It's a small world, five of you here from one college."

As soon as he said it, he knew. She had to be from West Point. They all were.

The vast majority of officers came from ROTC programs, but even if there were sixteen ROTC officers in a unit, they would most likely be from sixteen different universities. There might be only three West Point officers in comparison, but they always seemed to know each other. For her to have found four college friends in this one apartment complex? Yeah. They had to be ring-knockers.

"We all went to West Point," she offered, oblivious to what was obvious.

Thane had checked her left hand earlier. No engagement ring. No wedding band. Now he looked at her right hand. No West Point ring.

She caught his look and held up her right hand, wiggling her bare fingers. "I don't wear the ring all the time. It's not a requirement, you know. You're not wearing your class ring today, either. I'll have to guess where you went to college. Let's see, South Carolina…maybe Clemson? Wait—not the Citadel? Tell me you're from anywhere but the Citadel." She made a horrified face.

She did it so comically, it made him laugh. The Citadel was a private college that ran itself like a military academy. Thane had never had the money to go to a private college, which was one of the reasons he'd enlisted in the army at eighteen. "Nothing that bad."

"I know. I was joking." She dropped her horrified face and beamed at him, looking relaxed in his towel and ready for a long chat. "You'd definitely be wearing a big, honking ring if you were. Everyone calls *us* ring-knockers, but have you seen a Citadel ring? You'd think they won the Super Bowl or something. So, where did you go to school?"

"Duke University." He'd been able to start there at age twenty, after two years of enlisted service had helped him win an ROTC scholarship.

"*North* Carolina. Tricky of you. And your ring?"

"I don't ever wear a college ring. I didn't buy one."

"Why not? Duke's such a prestigious school."

"Now you're just flattering me. I like it."

She laughed, but she was still looking at him expectantly.

"I don't know why I didn't buy one. It's not really a big deal there."

She studied him. "That's interesting, that rings aren't a big deal at a big school like Duke. I try to imagine what life would have been like if I'd gone to regular college. Is it really like *Animal House*?"

"Not even close."

"Ever been to a toga party?"

He started to say no, but caught himself. "Actually, I have."

She wanted to know all about it. They talked, they told each other the little stories that made up their college lives. She was so enthusiastic about everything he told her, not like a standoffish, elite academy snob at all. It was surprising, the amount of college experiences she *hadn't* had. No fraternities or sororities. No weekend jobs at a local pizza place. No one already so drunk at two in the afternoon that they fell asleep in a dorm elevator. Hell—she hadn't lived in a dorm. She told him stories about daring Friday nights spent cleaning the barracks after taps in absolute darkness, so they'd pass Saturday Morning Inspections.

But she was so damned happy. Her buddies were really enjoying themselves, too, as if free beer and an apartment pool party were a vacation in the Bahamas. As usual, every West Pointer here seemed to know each other automatically, something that was at least mildly annoying to the rest of the army's officer corps. But talking to Chloe, Thane could see that there wasn't any mysterious network of ring-knockers. The West Pointers always seemed to already know each other because they *did* already know each other. They'd had no one else to get to know for four solid years.

Now that four years of a rather stringent life was over,

it sounded like Chloe was ready to do and see everything there was to do and see here in Killeen and Austin—and life. Thane was going to love being the man who did and saw everything with her.

There was no doubt in his mind that this was a woman who was worth dating, worth spending all his time with—hell, a woman worth *courting*. An hour talking with her in the shade felt like they were catching each other up on their lives before this day. From this day on, they would go out and experience things together. Chloe was terrific, all of her, inside and out, body and sharp mind and outgoing personality, this charming lieutenant from West Point.

It gave him hope for the new fourth platoon leader at work. Maybe the rookie West Pointer they were getting at the 584th wouldn't be so bad, either, the new female lieutenant his platoon sergeant had told him was…

Thane kept smiling as Chloe talked, but he took a long drink of his beer. Swallowed.

How many women went to West Point? Not many. If the army was roughly 15 percent female, then he'd bet West Point was about the same. Chloe would probably know the new platoon leader. So would Bill and Marcus and the other two guys. Right?

Another sip of beer. Another hard swallow.

For the first time, he wondered which branch Chloe was in. Somehow, he'd been thinking she must be in the same branch as her friends. A cluster of five new Signal Corps officers, or a new slate of field artillery officers, all reporting to duty at Fort Hood at the same time. Right?

Not likely. They didn't know each other from going to one branch's Basic Officer Leadership Course. They knew each other from earlier than that. They'd probably been surprised to see each other today because they'd graduated last May and then scattered to five different courses in five different branches of the army.

He pushed it to the back of his mind. Chloe's branch and

his branch would come up in conversation. There was no rush. They weren't doing anything wrong. There were no regulations against eating a hot dog at an apartment pool with anybody.

"Here, I'm dry enough. Let me spread out your towel so it will dry." Chloe stood up and untucked the towel knot. In one easy move, she peeled off the damp towel and swirled it like a cape to lay across the back of the chair.

Thane stopped thinking. She was all but nude on the other side of the table, not two feet away from him, flat stomach and sexy belly button at his eye level. He must look like a cartoon character, eyes bugging out of his head, mouth hanging open, tongue hanging out. Or else he looked like a stoic army officer, face devoid of expression. He hoped the latter. Cartoon on the inside, stoic on the outside. Overwhelmed.

Had she dropped that towel to overwhelm him intentionally? He managed to look up to her face, but no. She was oblivious, bending over in those bikini bottoms—holy hell, what a body—to grab her chair by its arms and drag it out from under the shade, chatting away the whole time. "It'll dry faster in the sun." She looked up to the sky to judge where the sun was and turned the chair so that it was sideways to his, then she flopped back into it.

"Ahh," she sighed, as she stretched out shapely legs and leaned her head back, closing her eyes as she tilted her face up to the sun. "I love this weather."

Was he supposed to speak? He cleared his throat. "You won't love it in July." She had her eyes closed; he could keep his eyes on her. "It hits one hundred and ten. Even higher."

She opened one eye to look at him. "Aren't you supposed to say, 'But it's a dry heat'?"

He grinned at her droll comment. "It's like living in an oven. Ovens don't have humidity, but they can roast a turkey."

She laughed. "I guess I'll find out myself in July. But today is perfect."

Yes, it is.

"It's so much better here than Leonard Wood."

He stayed perfectly still. He didn't even take a breath as the bottom dropped out of his world. Fort Leonard Wood. Home of the Military Police Corps. The one post that trained every damned MP in the whole damned army. Damn it, she was an MP.

She might be assigned to a different company. As long as we aren't in the same company...

They couldn't date if they were in the same *unit*. There were three MP companies in his battalion. As long as she wasn't in his battalion, then...

"It got below forty the night before I left Leonard Wood. I had enough of frozen winters at West Point. I picked Fort Hood because it wouldn't snow here. I didn't expect it to still be warm enough to sit by a pool, though. Life is good."

There was no other MP battalion here for her to belong to. The next level up was the 89th MP Brigade, headquartered here at Hood. Maybe she was assigned to brigade headquarters, maybe...

Maybe he was kidding himself.

Fourth platoon was getting a female West Pointer on Monday. West Pointers were a small percentage of all army officers; women from West Point were even more rare. There would be no other female West Point officers leaving Fort Leonard Wood and arriving at Fort Hood this week. Not another one this year. The woman Thane wanted to take to the movies just for the pleasure of having her company, the woman he was staring at, lusting over right this second, had to be Second Lieutenant—

"Michaels!" A man barked out the name from the other side of the pool deck's fence like an angry drill sergeant.

Chloe jerked upright and whipped around in her chair, blinking in the sun, her face a solid mix of anger and bewilderment. Thane stood up, ready to step in. Who the hell did this guy think he was?

Then Chloe made a little happy yelp of a noise and jumped to her feet. She nearly ran the few feet to the chest-high fence, but when Thane expected her to throw her arms around the man she obviously knew and was obviously happy to see, she came to a stop just before him and clasped her hands behind her back.

"It's so good to see you, sir. I didn't know you were at Hood."

"Come here. You're not a cadet. You can call me Greg." The man reached over the fence and yanked Chloe into his arms.

Thane realized he was clenching his jaw. All these old friends sure didn't miss the chance to hug her in her bikini. How many old friends could a woman have who'd lived here only a week?

Apparently, a half dozen or more, when the woman had graduated from West Point.

West Point. *Michaels.*

Fraternization. Court-martials.

Thane hadn't hugged Chloe yet. He never would.

Chloe turned to him. She wanted him to meet her old friend. It hurt Thane's heart. She was opening up her life to him, welcoming him in, because she still thought he was an interesting man. She still thought they were new friends and on their way to being more, to dinners and movies and a first kiss good-night.

They weren't.

It was all he could do to keep going through the motions. This Greg guy had to be about his age, twenty-five or -six, yet Chloe acted as though Greg far outranked her. Thane shook hands. With his gut churning, he made polite conversation. "Another West Point classmate?"

"Oh—no, a classmate is someone in your graduating class. Greg was a firstie—a senior—when I was a plebe. Not even a plebe yet. He was my CO for Beast Barracks."

"Beast Barracks is basic training at West Point," Greg

explained, bending forward to brace his arms on the fence, settling in for a chat. Yeah. Who wouldn't stop and chat with Chloe?

"I've heard the term," Thane said neutrally. He felt trapped. He needed to break up with a woman the same day he'd met her. It was the last thing in the world he wanted to do.

"He was scarier than the drill sergeant in *Full Metal Jacket* during Beast," Chloe said, "but he watched out for us the rest of the year."

"Hazed her a little bit, but she was a stubborn little cuss. Couldn't break her." Greg smiled at Chloe. "Looks like you turned out just fine."

Thane didn't miss this Greg guy checking out the way his *plebe* looked now, four years later. Thane couldn't date Chloe, and it was going to kill him to watch her date anyone else.

"So, how do you two know each other?" Greg asked. At least Chloe's former cadet CO had the decency to see if the coast was clear before putting a move on her.

Chloe smiled at Thane, happiness that killed him, then did an adorable little duck of her chin, although she was the last person he'd expect to be shy. "We just met today. He's going to show me around town sometime."

No, I'm not. So sorry, Chloe. So very damned sorry.

He kept going through all the motions, listening to them reminisce for a polite amount of time before excusing himself to get a beer, and did anyone else want one? No?

Thane stood at the keg for a red plastic cup of beer he didn't even want, trying to brace himself against the hurt he was going to cause when he told Chloe this whole day had been a big mistake, when out of the corner of his eye, he saw a man in uniform heading toward the parking lot, carrying a black MP bulletproof vest. Thane snapped out of his pity party. He could mourn his disappointed heart later. Right now, he needed to avoid immediate trouble.

The man walking by the pool's fence was a platoon leader from one of the other MP companies in the battalion. He was in his ACUs and carrying a thermos in one hand, that black vest in the other, obviously on his way to take over as duty officer. He spotted Thane and raised the thermos in a brief wave. "Wish me luck. Saturday night and a full moon. Phillips owes me a case of beer for covering this shift for him."

Thane did the lift-of-the-chin greeting, all he could manage as dread filled his chest. That had been a close call. Too close. Five minutes sooner, and that lieutenant would have seen Thane smiling and laughing and sitting nice and close at a cozy table for two *with his fellow platoon leader*. And it was far too true that it didn't always matter what you were doing, it mattered what it *looked* like you were doing, and that would have looked bad. If Chloe arrived at the battalion Monday morning and that lieutenant had recognized her as the girl Thane had been cozying up to at the pool, the rumor mill would have exploded like a bomb detonating.

Legally, they'd done absolutely nothing wrong. Thane would be able to stand in front of the CO and honestly tell him he and Lieutenant Michaels had only talked. But the gossip surrounding that closed-door meeting would tarnish a reputation, and Thane already knew it would be her reputation that got tarnished far worse than his, as unfair as that would be. Women were just under greater scrutiny. She'd be toast before she even got to put her name on their office door. What made a man look like a stud would make a woman look like…

Yeah. She'd start out deep in a hole that she hadn't dug. He couldn't do that to her.

He needed to leave ASAP, before more people saw them together. This situation was like a hand grenade that had had its safety pin pulled and was now primed to explode. The second Thane could get Chloe alone, he'd tell her they were assigned to the same company. He could slide the safety pin back into place and set the hand grenade down safely. Nothing had to explode. He'd leave Chloe here where he'd found her, with her classmates and her former cadet CO, and he'd go back to his apartment, shut the door and resume his regular routine. Alone.

Alone, damn it, with no Chloe to wine and dine and talk to.

Ballerina Baby.

Not totally alone. Ballerina would be waiting to hear from him. The only safe person he'd had to talk to before this pool party was still the only safe person he had to talk to. How could he explain this whole debacle to her without explaining that he was in the military, with all the ins and outs of rank and fraternization? He couldn't. He was going to have to deal with the hope and grief of finding and losing a wonderful woman all on his own.

Thane turned to see if Chloe was back at their table, so he could get this conversation over with before they were busted. She wasn't at the table and she wasn't by the fence. She was probably near the grill, talking to one of the golden retrievers. Thane walked in the opposite direction, yanking his towel off the back of her chair as he passed it, heading toward the pool house with its restrooms and dinky outdoor shower. His chair was in the shade of the pool house, the chair he'd dropped his stuff on eons ago, before he'd ever seen Lieutenant Michaels and her happy smile. If he'd known then what he knew now…

He would've stayed in his apartment and talked to Ballerina.

He scuffed on his flip-flops. He needed to be ready to leave as soon as he filled Chloe in. The lieutenant they'd just missed by sheer luck wasn't the only MP living in the entire six-building complex.

"Hey, Lieutenant Carter."

And there was another. Thane turned around slowly. An MP, one of the NCOs from his own company, was being friendly. Specifically, it was Staff Sergeant Gevahr, who was a squad leader in fourth platoon. Chloe's platoon. Sergeant Gevahr would directly report to Chloe on Monday.

Thane needed to handle this grenade very carefully. He prayed Chloe wouldn't spot him and come over to stand by his side while he talked with her squad leader. If she didn't come over, if the sergeant had just arrived and if Thane could leave immediately, then there'd be nothing for the sergeant to see. *If* the sergeant hadn't seen them together yet. If he already had...

If he already had, then when Staff Sergeant Gevahr met his new platoon leader on Monday, he was going to recognize her and that grenade would explode.

Thane pulled his apartment keys out of the pocket of his board shorts, making it clear he was on his way out. "Hey, Staff Sergeant. What's up?"

Staff Sergeant Gevahr only started to laugh. "I was going to ask you that, sir. I was going to come over and say hi at least an hour ago, but it didn't look like you'd appreciate the interruption. Who's the new girlfriend, sir?"

The grenade was about to explode.

Chapter Five

Chloe felt like she just might explode with happiness.

As she washed her hands in the pool house bathroom, she looked at herself in the mirror over the sink. Who cared about the half-wet hair, drying without the benefit of a comb? Chloe couldn't stop smiling.

Thane. Thane, Thane, Thane…

She'd never been so crazy over a man so quickly. The endorphin rush was like a runner's high, but without the miles of exertion one had to go through first to reach that point. The burst of adrenaline was like the one a child felt on Christmas morning, not the kind a soldier felt during a dangerous live-fire exercise. She glanced in the mirror again. Still smiling. She couldn't stop—because Thane felt the same way about her. She knew that, because he wasn't afraid to say he liked her.

Just like Drummer.

Her heart pounded for a moment, a guilty beat.

What was she going to tell Drummer about their little experiment? That it was a smashing success? That she'd found more than a friend? She wouldn't have a chance to tell Drummer about it until much later, because Thane had made it plain that he wanted to keep spending his time with her *today*. He wasn't going to do that nonsense where a man asked for her number and then waited three days or a whole week before calling, all in an effort to not appear desperate.

Thane wasn't a desperate man. Just the opposite: he knew what he wanted, and he wasn't afraid to come and get it.

Her heart pounded again, from a better emotion this time. She'd been away from Thane for at least ten minutes. Seeing Cadet Towers—now Lieutenant Towers—*Greg*—had been nice, but Chloe wanted to be with Thane instead.

She finished drying her hands on a paper towel and went

to grasp the swinging door's handle just as someone else pushed it in toward her. A woman with an empty stroller struggled in the doorway, a baby on her hip and a toddler dragging behind. Chloe stepped back and held the door open as they crowded into the little two-stall space.

Outside, she heard a man's voice. "Girlfriend? Give me a break, Staff Sergeant."

It was Thane talking. He used a different tone of voice talking with a man than he did with her, but she recognized his voice, that barely there Southern drawl. She'd been listening to that voice all afternoon, and she was looking forward to listening to it for weeks to come. Months. Years. All right, it was too soon to be thinking in years, but this man was really something special.

She was smiling at the thought when Thane said, "I don't stick with one woman very long."

Oh.

That was before he'd met her, though, right? She was a new person, maybe a new chapter in his life…but still, he really didn't sound like himself. He sounded kind of arrogant.

Outside, a different male voice said, "Every man says that, sir, until he meets—"

Inside, the mother told her toddler to get up from the floor. "It's dirty. Yucky."

The same man sounded like he was laughing. "—change that real quick. I've been watching you talk to that girl all day. Just one girl, sir. Just one."

"Talking," Thane emphasized with a definite scoff in his tone. "When all I do is talk, there's your clue."

Ouch.

Chloe stayed where she was, wedged by the sink as she kept holding the door open with one hand. She felt like she'd missed something. Thane was talking about some other girl, surely.

"Now, sir, I was born at night, but it wasn't last night.

A man doesn't sit at a little tiny table with a woman for a whole afternoon—"

The mother's voice was an octave higher. "Get off the floor, Mattie. Now."

There was a moment of silence as the last of the *now* echoed off the tile.

Thane spoke. "Did you see her face?"

"Well…no, sir." The man sounded just a little bit hesitant at the question.

That had been kind of a weird question. *Did you see her face?* Chloe looked at her face in the mirror. Nothing weird to see there.

"She had her back to me, sir. But that's a fine-looking back, if you don't mind me saying so, and judging from your face, the front view must be at least as good as the back view."

Chloe held her breath.

Thane didn't say anything for the longest moment. "You've been here a while, then. Did I catch you on your way out?"

"Yes, sir, but—"

"Great. I'm leaving, too. Let's go."

"But, sir. What about your lady friend?"

Thane lowered his voice, but she could still hear him. "She's not a friend, and she's definitely not my lady. You didn't see her face. If you had, you'd fully appreciate why I'm making an escape with you."

It was a punch to Chloe's gut, a blow that did real damage because she hadn't been prepared for it at all.

"You sure were spending a lot of time with her—"

"Do you see any other single women around here? I had to take what I could get. Trust me, I can't take anymore, so do me a favor and let me walk out in front of you. Don't even look toward her. If she turns around, I don't want her to see anything except your back, hiding mine. I appreciate the cover…"

Their voices faded away.

How could she have been so wrong? How could she have so completely misjudged him?

The door slipped out of her hand and swung gently closed. She stood there, paralyzed, until she realized she was staring at herself in the mirror. There was nothing wrong with her face. There was nothing—it couldn't have been Thane. It wasn't Thane speaking.

She grabbed for the door handle and yanked it open. Among the mostly stationary folks mingling on the pool deck, two men were moving briskly, heading directly for the gate. One was a stranger. The other was Thane, head high, shoulders back, her towel—his towel—thrown over one shoulder. Leaving without saying goodbye. Leaving without a word of explanation.

If you'd seen her face... I'm making an escape.

She fell back against the wall with the pain of it. He'd liked her. He'd liked her as much as she'd liked him. Why would he say such a cruel thing?

Chloe knew, objectively, that she didn't have an ugly face, but his words tapped into years of insecurities. There was still plenty of simmering resentment out there against women in the military, too many "jokes" about how they must all be ugly gorillas, how they all must hate men, how they all must be whores. Women too ugly for any man to sleep with, yet who slept with numerous men—all contradictions, all cruel. And it didn't matter when Chloe told herself it was all false, not when she'd heard it, or hints of it, or felt it behind her back every week and month and year. Year after year since the year she'd turned eighteen.

That seed of doubt could be consciously squashed, but it was still there, that tiny bit of herself that wondered not only if she was less than a woman, but if there was something wrong with her for wanting to serve her country.

The tiled wall hadn't held her up. She vaguely realized she'd slid down and was hunkered down on her haunches.

"Yucky." The toddler chewed on her fingers as she stood eye to eye with Chloe. "Yucky."

"Mattie, come here. Leave the nice lady alone." The mother's voice had turned gentler as she glanced sympathetically at Chloe while buckling her infant into the stroller.

"Oh—no, it's all right." Chloe rose up again, feeling the burn in her thighs from the squat. "Here, let me get the door for you."

She followed the woman and children out of the bathroom. She surveyed the pool scene, but she didn't want to stay here, not even with friends from West Point.

Friends. One of them had been her friend while they were cadets. Two of them were more like acquaintances whom she'd had in a class or two. Greg Towers had been too many years ahead of her to be a friend, and Keith had surprised her by being friendly to her today, because, frankly, he'd been an ass at school.

If she called being body-slammed into a pool "friendly," that is. She'd played it off because that's what one had to do. Deflect, act like you can handle anything, pretend they didn't upset you. She was a pro at that. She had to be to survive.

Chloe didn't run, but she didn't waste any time, either. She stalked over to her stuff, unrolled the yellow dress and caught her cell phone case, then started pulling the sundress over her head as she headed toward the gate. Anger was building inside her. Fury. All she wanted was to be alone. She couldn't wait to lock herself back in her apartment. She didn't want to talk to another human being for the rest of the weekend—no one except Drummer.

He was the only one who'd understand.

Thank God she had someone who'd understand, because she surely didn't have someone who would tell her about toga parties and smile at her stories and take her to see a movie.

She made it all the way to apartment 401 before the fury deserted her and left tears in its place.

* * *

What would you do if you were me?

Chloe hit the enter key and chomped down hard on another frozen grape, her twentieth, at least. Fresh fruit was her current favorite comfort food. Strawberries, blueberries, peaches—anything that she'd had to live without for the last four and a half years.

The dining facility at Leonard Wood had served bananas and oranges. So had the mess hall at West Point. Those fruits were kept in stock because they were hardy, and they came with their own thick skins. She was done with bananas and oranges. She was sick of having a thick skin.

Because right now, I'm just stress-eating grapes. Have you ever put grapes in the freezer? Amazing. They stop just short of turning into ice cubes.

She didn't care if dudes didn't talk about food cravings. She was talking to Drummer without a filter today. He was either her friend or he wasn't. If he couldn't handle her online, then it would be best if he just disappeared.

Like Thane had.

She popped another grape in her mouth.

Blue words came across her screen. I thought tater tots were your comfort food of choice.

Good. Drummer could handle her even when she didn't weigh every word.

The tots are all dead, remember? I've moved on. Grapes are my victims now.

Chloe looked at her laptop screen with its jaunty little lines of pink and blue type. She sounded so jaunty herself, didn't she? Tots and grapes, ha ha ha.

She was brokenhearted.

You're doing better than I am, Drummer wrote. *I'm halfway through a cholesterol-filled pepperoni pizza. No one can fault you for grapes. No one can fault you for anything. What would I do if I were you? I'd look in the mirror and remind myself that I'm smart enough, I'm good enough, and gosh darn it, people like me.*

She snorted. *Saturday Night Live (too easy).*

(Of course it was easy, but you've had a hard day.) Then I'd come up with a plan for what to do if I should run into friends who are not really friends again.

Chloe had chickened out. She'd told Drummer that she regretted going to her party, but when he'd asked why, she'd focused on Keith's friendliness-that-wasn't-really-friendliness. The more she thought about it, the more aggressive she realized Keith's poolside tackle had been. There was a time and a place for aggressiveness. Hand-to-hand combat training? Check. Slamming a woman into the water who'd just arrived at a party? Wrong.

But even there, she hadn't given Drummer the ugly truth. It made her sound so wimpy, that she'd been dunked—hard—and left to look like a drowned rat the rest of the party, yet she hadn't done anything to defend herself except laugh it off.

Instead, she'd told Drummer something vague, saying someone who wasn't really a friend had gotten in a cheap shot. So much for her determination to talk to Drummer without a filter. She couldn't imagine what Drummer would think if she told him it was an actual *physical* cheap shot, being tackled from behind.

It was a no-win situation, anyway. She tried to explain that much to Drummer. *How do you come up with a plan? It's not like there are many options. You either complain or you laugh it off. I went with laugh it off this time, which made everyone around me happy and kept the party mood going.*

If I'd complained...well, you get labeled as a complainer or a whiner and no one wants to be around that. They sure won't line up to volunteer to take you to the airport if they think they'll be stuck in a car with a whiner.

Give me a little more information on what went down today. I'll help you brainstorm some options.

No. No specifics, remember? This anonymity thing is working for us.

Drummer sent her an eye-roll emoji. Okay. So, you ran into someone you thought was a friend and then they were not. What is your goal in life?

You mean my goal with this not-a-friend? I don't have one. I'm fine with him—or her—not being my friend.

No, I mean your goal in life. All of life. Big life.

Big life? She stuffed the last two grapes into her mouth at once. They were so cold, they hurt.

Life goals she had, but they were all specific and clearly defined: to serve her nation as an officer in the MP Corps. To be a platoon leader, to take care of her troops and to set a good example for those she led. She couldn't tell Drummer any of those goals and still keep any anonymity.

All of her previous goals had been equally specific. As a cadet, she'd aimed for grades that would rank her high enough in her class to get her first choice of branch and then her first choice of post, somewhere snow-free. Even in high school, she'd had specific goals on the school track team—earning a varsity letter was a must for her academy dream. She'd had goals on the SAT test—she needed to at least match the average of new cadets to become one herself.

She looked around her mostly empty apartment, the one

that would never be inspected, as she sat on her new couch that was as red as a rose. She'd met her past goals. She felt trained and ready to accomplish her future military service goals. But what was her real goal in life? Big life?

I want to be happy. She hit Send before she could censor herself.

Good. The blue answer was immediate. Drummer thought something as vague as happiness was a good goal? That made her feel marginally better.

Let's measure your options by whether or not they'll make you happy. One option is to laugh it off. You tried that today, and it didn't make you happy, right?

Nope. It was a reflex at the time, but now I feel like a doormat.

Doormats are not happy. But Ballerina, listen. Don't be so hard on yourself for laughing it off. You tried a viable option to handling unwanted attention, one that must have worked in the past or it wouldn't have been your default, right?

Chloe stopped crunching her grapes for a moment. How did he do that? How did Drummer know everything about her?

But that option didn't sit well with you, so let's move on to option two. You could ignore this person, pretend you didn't see him/her, or pretend you didn't hear him/her. Next time you see this person, will ignoring her make you happy?

Maybe.

Maybe's not good enough, BB. This is your one and only life. Maybe means no, ignoring this person isn't going to make you happy. And you already tried laughing off her joke that was really an insult. That's a no. So, option three, you could confront this person. Will telling her off make you happy?

Maybe. It was a him, by the way, not a her. I couldn't really respond. He just got in his hit and walked away before I could answer.

> Keith had jumped out of the pool and headed for the keg. Whatever.
> Thane had gotten in his hit—*Did you see her face?*—and left, too.
> The hurt of Thane's hit was so fresh, still shocking in its cruelty. Chloe let the fury come in to push the hurt away, typing with hard hits on the keys. I don't know if confrontation will make me happy, but it will keep me from feeling like I feel tonight, which is basically powerless. I've put up with a lot of crap so far in life, and I'm reaching a point of boiling over. She hit the send key so hard, her finger stung.

Let's come up with a plan, then. Your default next time, if there is a next time, will be to confront him. When you boil over, you don't want to be burned. You want to keep that steam directed to the correct target, right? The key will be confronting him in a way that won't make you look bad to anyone else. Wouldn't want you to hurt your reputation at your job, for example.

> Keith was not her target. Chloe had dealt with him and his kind for years. But if she ran into Thane someday in the parking lot, she didn't want to pretend she didn't see him and skitter away.

Right. Plan C—controlled confrontation. I'm ready.

Chapter Six

"Good evening, ma'am."

"Good evening, Sergeant First Class." Chloe set her black bulletproof vest on the edge of the watch commander's desk. The police station was built for efficiency, not beauty, especially here in the back of the building, with the briefing rooms and holding cells. The decor was little more than metal lockers and functional, plain furniture.

There was something exciting about it, though, with its hot links to fire stations and its wall maps delineating all their areas of responsibility across three counties in Central Texas. Everything was plain and boring, yet everything was in a state of readiness. There was a palpable sense that all the calm and order could change in a moment, and the people in this building knew they would be the quickest to respond, the first to help. *Assist-Protect-Defend.*

Calm and order were very much the order of the day—or evening. Sunday evening at the police station was far quieter than Friday night had been. Chloe was ready to go, though. Tonight was her second ride-along with the duty officer, her chance to keep learning the post's layout—really, to keep learning the whole job. She knew all the official radio communication standards, for example, but on Friday night, she'd had a hard time following the sound of the dispatcher coming over the radio at real speed in the patrol car. The most important thing she'd caught was that the officer on duty was 310, or three-ten. When dispatch said the words *three-ten*, she needed to pay attention. When another MP requested that three-ten come by for support, that meant her.

Well, it meant the duty officer. Plus her, the ride-along. And their driver, of course. Friday night the driver had been a specialist from first platoon. A specialist was the next rank up from a private first class, making him an enlisted man with a couple of years of service under his belt. With the driver and the real duty officer in the front seats of the patrol car, she'd sat in the back, trying not to think about how many drunks or drug addicts had sat where she was sitting. It was hard to see exactly which streets the patrol car was taking and hard to hear the radio as well from the back seat, but that was the only option there was. She'd just suck it up and keep doing her best from the back seat tonight.

It was a relief to be working at a real-world task tonight. Memorizing the layout of an entire town would surely keep her mind busy. She'd had too much time to think since yesterday's pool party. Talking to Drummer hadn't even been a distraction, because whether Drummer knew it or not, Thane had been the subject of their conversation. There was nothing she could do alone in her apartment that kept her mind off Thane.

She'd tried. The army had provided shipping for her move to Texas, and her stuff had arrived. But unpacking boxes when she'd been looking forward to a date with a handsome man had been depressing. From school, she'd shipped to herself a footlocker of cadet uniforms that she'd never wear again and the world's heaviest boxes of textbooks that she'd never read again. The army had authorized one shipment from her "home of record," too, which was her parents' house. Her parents had given her the dresser and bed she'd had since childhood. It was another twin bed, of course, but one that didn't have to be made up with a gray blanket in hospital corners. She'd bought a new bedspread at the PX, a grown-up coverlet in soothing shades of blue and green, but still, her childhood bedroom furniture made her a little homesick.

Her mom had also given her some spare pots and pans, so Chloe had tried cooking to keep herself busy. She'd moved from healthy grapes to the ultimate comfort food, hot and rich macaroni and cheese, yet eating straight from the casserole dish as it sat on a footlocker was a poor substitute for dinner at a restaurant, sitting across a real table from a handsome man.

And, damn him, Thane was a handsome man. A jerk, but handsome. He had dark hair and light eyes, a mouth that she'd imagined kissing hers, plus shoulders and biceps and chest muscles all deliciously defined.

"Lieutenant Carter is the officer on duty tonight, ma'am." The watch commander was a senior NCO, the most senior one working tonight, the same man she'd met on Friday's ride-along. The watch commander stayed at the station to oversee everything from walk-ins to the holding cells to the dispatchers. "I told him you'd be riding along. He said he'd wait outside for you. Just through the briefing room and out that back door."

Chloe put on her protective vest, getting it situated above the thick black belt that held her sidearm in its holster. "No briefing today?"

"The NCOs handle that, ma'am. It's up to the lieutenant if he wants to be there or not."

Lieutenant Salvatore had stood in the back of the briefing room Friday. Chloe guessed this Lieutenant Carter did things differently. She nodded at the watch commander and headed through the empty briefing room, tugging the black vest down. The bright white letters spelling *Military Police* across her chest made it clear to good guys and bad guys alike exactly who she was on any scene, something that could otherwise be confusing when law enforcement and perpetrators were often all wearing the same camouflage uniforms. It gave her the odd sensation of wearing a half shirt, because the heavy part of the vest didn't cover the lower part of her stomach.

She pulled her patrol cap out of her pocket and slid it on so it sat properly, just above her low ballerina bun. Then she was out the door, into the twilight. A patrol car was parked off to the side, a male lieutenant leaning against it, arms crossed over his chest, studying the ground at his feet. She adjusted the brim of her hat just so with one hand and tugged down the black vest quickly with her other, still annoyed at that bare-belly sensation.

"You must be Lieutenant Carter," she said in a voice to carry over the several paces of asphalt between them.

He lifted his head and looked at her from under the brim of his patrol cap.

She stopped walking.

The silence between them went on too long as a thousand thoughts raced through her head.

Someone had to say something. She did. "Are you kidding me?"

He just kept his eyes on her, those light-colored eyes, his expression as grim as a man at a funeral. Grim, but not surprised.

Drummer's advice was fresh in her mind. Option one: she could be polite, say *gee, isn't this awkward*, laugh, and pretend everything was okay. *It didn't sit well with you, Ballerina.*

Option two: she could ignore him. Impossible, since he was an MP and on duty tonight. *It won't make you happy.*

Option three: controlled confrontation.

She didn't think happiness was really going to be the outcome, but Drummer had been right, the other two options would leave her seething with resentment toward Thane and disappointed with herself. She wasn't going to smile and pretend everything was okay.

Her heart was pounding underneath all the layers that were supposed to protect her: vest, armor plates, ACU jacket, tan T-shirt, sports bra. There was no protection against emotions. Her heart still took the hit of seeing his handsome face again, so unexpectedly, the face she'd smiled with, flirted with, trusted…all while he'd been finding her face not good enough. He'd made her hope for more. He'd made her want him.

Bastard.

She let fury squash the heartache and took a minute, gaze locked with his, to consider what to say. She'd been caught off guard, but Thane was not shocked to see her at all.

She started there. "You're not surprised to see me."

"Hi, Chloe."

"You knew? You knew we were both MPs? We're both—hang on. Are you in my company?" She was pretty certain Salvatore had said that just the lieutenants from the 584th were taking shifts this month.

He nodded solemnly. "I'm first platoon. You're fourth."

She saw red. But she also saw the white badge on his black vest, the white and green patrol car he leaned against, and her awareness of her situation kept her in control. That, and her four years of military training. She was standing outside a police station, in uniform. Soldiers, other MPs, were coming and going through the same side door she'd used. She could have happily gotten in Thane's face like she was hazing a plebe, but she wouldn't do anything to draw attention to the two of them. She wasn't going to boil over and burn herself.

She took those last steps to stand in front of him and crossed her arms over her chest as he uncrossed his. He stayed where he was, leaning against the driver's side door. In silence, she stared him down, using the same iron glare she would have used if he'd been a plebe, and she'd ordered him to stand at attention with his back against a barracks wall, braced as he struggled to recite a long passage of General MacArthur's words correctly to the last syllable.

Thane looked away. He took his patrol cap off, smoothed his hand up the back of his hair, put the cap back on. "I didn't know you were riding with me tonight. I'm just glad someone mentioned it in time for me to get out here before you arrived. I didn't want anyone in the station to see your shock."

"You sunovabitch."

He looked back at her.

She kept her voice low, just between the two of them.

"You know what would have prevented a lot of shock? If you'd introduced yourself properly at the pool."

"I didn't know who you were. Not right away."

"When did you know?" *Was it before or after you decided my face was too ugly for you?*

"You mentioned Leonard Wood while we were talking."

"And you kept talking to me?"

"I—" Whatever words he'd been about to say got stuck in his throat.

"You kept talking to me. You never bothered to say you'd been to Leonard Wood, too, or that you were an MP, too."

"I was going to."

"But you didn't. Didn't fraternization occur to you?"

"Yes."

"You were toying with my career." *And my heart.*

Thane pushed away from the patrol car and stood over her. She wasn't a short woman, but he still was taller by several inches. If he thought she was going to be unnerved by the way he looked down at her, if he thought she'd blink or back away even a half step, then he truly had no idea where she'd lived or what she'd been through to make second lieutenant.

"I can't toy with your career without toying with my own," he said.

"True. I don't know what makes a person take the kind of risk you took, but I didn't choose to take that risk. Maybe it gives you a thrill to push the envelope and not get caught, but I worked too hard to be standing right where I am today to risk it all like that. Your little game isn't fun when it can hurt someone else."

"There was no game. I didn't know the new LT's name was Chloe, only Michaels." He paused. "It was never a game."

She blinked. It was never a game? He spoke so sincerely, trying to soothe her feelings now, wanting her to think the only reason he'd dumped her stone-cold was because he'd figured out they were going to be in the same unit.

Oh, how she would have loved to have believed that. Her heart wouldn't hurt so much if she could fool herself into thinking his heart had been involved, as well. She would've been gullible enough to believe him right now, too, if she hadn't opened a bathroom door and heard the truth. *When all I do is talk to a woman, there's your clue. I had to take what I could get.*

He'd been playing games, all right. He'd left without a backward glance once she'd agreed to go out with him. He was the kind of man who was all about the chase. The hunt. The kind of guy who would win a woman's heart just to prove he could, then dump her. How many Monday mornings in the cadet mess hall had she spent listening to the guys describe their weekend conquests, bragging about how they'd charmed a woman, how they'd looked her in the eye and used the line *I really love you* just to get her into bed? Chloe knew that game.

Fool me once, shame on you. Fool me twice...

There'd be no second time. She was completely immune to Thane's nice-guy act. He'd made sure of that with the way he'd walked out.

"Yeah, look, Thane. *Carter.* Cut the crap. From this point on, it's got to be all work and no play. No more of your games. Don't bother testing out your charm on me. We work together, nothing else. Can you handle that?"

An NCO in a black MP vest called over them. "Lieutenant Carter, we're ready to go if you are, sir."

In icy silence, Thane stepped around her to head across the parking lot toward a formation of about twenty soldiers, lined up in two rows.

Chloe turned to follow.

Thane stayed a half step ahead of her as they walked, but after a few strides, he looked at her over his shoulder and spoke in a voice that was quiet but dripping with scorn. "Here's the thing, Michaels. I'm ahead of you in every way. You don't have the knowledge I do of this post, you don't know how the company operates and you have zero real-world experience in law enforcement. The question isn't can I handle you. The question is, can you keep up with me?"

The NCO-in-charge was addressing his two rows of MPs as Thane stood off to the side with Chloe—Lieutenant Michaels—standing at his shoulder like a shadow.

All work and no play. Can you handle that?

Definitely. He'd expected her to be shocked. He deserved a medal for making sure she wouldn't be shocked in front of the people she'd have to work with from now on. He'd been thoughtful, damn it, having her meet him outside. She'd used the privacy he'd given her to chew him out.

He'd expected her to be hurt. Instead, she'd zeroed right in on the specifics like a detective. When had he known and why hadn't he spoken up sooner?

He slid her a look as the NCO read off the list of vehicles for which alerts had been issued. Chloe was listening. There was no smile. She didn't radiate happiness. In fact, she looked fairly fierce, concentrating on descriptions of stolen cars and vehicles suspected of being involved in crimes. Thane had a feeling he could ask her to list all the vehicles' makes and models when the NCO was done, and she'd spit them right out.

Because she was sharp.

She was also beautiful.

Both were reasons why he hadn't leaned forward at that little patio table and said, "Leonard Wood? Are you an MP? So am I."

It should have been the easiest, most obvious thing to do. But he'd sat there, devastated. In denial. Mentally grasping at straws, looking for a way for the truth not to be true.

He'd felt the loss of a relationship that would never be, but, obviously, she hadn't. *Cut the crap.* All work and no play for Michaels and Carter was how she wanted it? It was exactly what she was going to get.

It was time to train the rookie. "Before every shift, we conduct PCCs just like we were leaving the wire downrange. PCC stands for pre-combat check."

"I know. You can inspect everyone while I stand here and watch, or it can take half as long if you take the front row and I take the back."

She wanted to conduct the inspection herself, with all the experience of a single ride-along under her belt? He almost had to admire that level of cockiness.

Fine. If she wanted to jump into the deep end of the pool, he'd let her.

Done with his briefing, the NCO called the two lines of waiting soldiers to attention, then turned to salute Thane.

Thane returned the salute and stood in front of the MPs. "I've got a ride-along tonight, Lieutenant Michaels. She'll be taking over fourth platoon, starting tomorrow."

That was enough of an explanation. He walked to the first soldier in the first line, and gestured for Michaels to start the second row.

Thane looked over each soldier from head to toe. He could tell in a glance if they had their uniforms on straight, if haircuts were in regulation, faces had been shaved, ACU trousers were properly bloused over their combat boots. Tonight, he was looking to make sure no one had tried to lighten their load by taking an armor plate out of its pocket on the black vest. He asked each soldier to turn on his flashlight, to show him they had latex gloves in a pocket, handcuff keys, their own military ID. All the while, he kept one eye on Michaels. She was doing the same.

Almost.

She was so damned sure of herself. She executed a sharp left face to step to the next soldier in line. He wanted to scoff at that level of drill and ceremony, one usually saved for formal events like changes of command in the regular army. It so clearly marked her as fresh out of West Point. He wanted to scoff, but she did it without any pretense, moving down her line as if proper military courtesies were as natural as breathing to her. On her, that strictly executed drill looked kind of cool.

Thane finished his row and waited off to the side of the formation for her to finish with her last soldier. "Everything good?" he asked her conversationally.

"Yes, s—" She caught herself almost calling him *sir*. She wasn't a cadet anymore, as her *friend* Greg had pointed out, but even the cocky Michaels forgot that now and then, apparently.

He managed not to smile at that little gaffe. He had a bigger mistake to point out. "You sure about that? Everyone has a working flashlight?"

"Of course everyone's got a flashlight. Do you require them to be on the belt or in a vest pocket?"

"Soldier's choice." Then he spoke so softly there was no way anyone in formation could hear him. "That's the kind of thing you should have asked before inspection, don't you think?"

He didn't give her a chance to respond. Instead, he took a step toward the formation and looked down her row. "Second row, take your flashlights out, turn them on and point them my way."

They did. One soldier, just one, had a flashlight that didn't light up.

These soldiers were from third platoon, but Thane knew them all by name. "Specialist Wesson, dead batteries? Come on, you know better."

The NCO was on it, dismissing Wesson to go inside and scrounge up either new batteries or borrow a working flashlight. With a quick exchange of salutes—proper but casual salutes, like real soldiers, not West Pointers—Thane turned over control of the personnel to the NCO, and headed to his patrol car. Michaels kept pace beside him, her chin still up despite the fact that he'd just taught her a lesson.

That was what he was here for. And if the lesson had been

taught in a way that she'd never forget, so much the better. He deserved a pat on the back for not rubbing it in her face with an *I told you so*. Little butter bar West Pointer, so sure she knew how to inspect the—

"You forgot to inspect one thing," she said.

"What's that?"

"Me."

"You're an officer. You have to police yourself."

"Fine. Then I have to tell you, since you didn't notice it, that I haven't drawn a radio yet."

Everyone else had one, a walkie-talkie style of radio with a cord that attached to a small, square speaker/microphone combination. Most MPs kept the speaker clipped on their shoulder, so they could hear and answer dispatch without having to take the bigger, clunkier radio off their belt.

Thane kept walking, but he glanced at her, trying not to look like he was inspecting her gear. The vest looked right. She had the standard sidearm, a nine-millimeter Beretta, in the same holster they all wore. Hers was on her right hip. She must be right-handed.

He had a fleeting memory of Saturday in the shade, of wanting to know every little detail about her. She was right-handed.

As if he cared.

"You don't need a radio." He sounded curt, even to himself.

"Yes, I do."

"You're either going to be in the car with its built-in radio, or you're going to be with me." Thane had a radio, of course. "Most of the initial dispatches are done through the computer. I'll angle it so you can see the screen."

"I need a radio so I can hear the *radio* traffic. If you haven't tried it before, let me tell you that it's hard to hear what's going on from the back seat. If I had a handheld unit, I'd be able to keep track better. It's easier to learn all the call signs and codes if you can hear all the call signs and codes."

Smart aleck. Thane kept walking toward the patrol car, away from the station where all the handheld radios were stored. "Not an issue. You won't be in the back seat tonight."

"You're going to take the back seat?" She seemed surprised, pleasantly surprised. "I appreciate that. It will be easier to get my bearings and see where we're going."

"I'm not sitting in the back." He was the officer on duty. He needed to see where the hell he was going more than she needed to be able to read street signs. "I'm driving."

"Lieutenant Salvatore had a driver. Specialist Baker, first platoon. He must be your soldier."

"During law enforcement rotations, the officers take different shifts than the enlisted. Our days are broken into twelve-hour shifts. Theirs are eight. They work three days on day shift, three on mids, three on nights, then get three days off. You won't be working with your own platoon most shifts."

"I know. I already got the basics. This isn't my first ride-along."

His first impression of her had been that she could be a Zen-master fitness and yoga instructor, happy with the world and her place in it. Now he watched her as she stalked away from him to head for the passenger door of the cruiser. Zen yoga? Not a chance.

Thane took his time walking up to his side of the car just to annoy her.

She kept talking. "I wasn't asking why you weren't working with a soldier from your own platoon. I was asking why you didn't have a driver. Is it up to each duty officer to decide if he wants a driver or not?"

"It's Sunday. Nothing happens on Sundays, so we don't put as many MPs on the road. When was your other ride-along?"

She opened her door and stood there, talking to him across the roof of the car, along the length of the blue-and-red light strip. "Friday night."

He opened his door. "On Fridays and Saturdays, everyone gets a partner."

Everyone got a partner at work, he meant. Thane's Saturday night after the pool party had been lonely as hell, but at least he'd had Ballerina to talk to about their wasted attempts to make real-life friends. Friday night, he hadn't even had that. Ballerina had made him laugh about tater tots and then run off for her late night, a late night she'd said she enjoyed. Without him.

"Tonight, Michaels, it's just you and me."

He got in the car and slammed his door.

Chapter Seven

Chloe got in the patrol car and slammed her door shut.

"What are you doing?" Thane demanded.

She had no patience for his high-handedness. "I'm getting in the car. What do you think I'm doing?"

"Getting in the car," he agreed. "Now you can get out of the car. In the real army, we don't go anywhere in any vehicle before we PMCS it. That's preventative maintenance checks and services. Since I'm the driver, I get to sit here while you walk around the vehicle and tell me if all the headlights and brake lights are working."

She jerked her car door open. "I know what the hell PMCS means." She got out and slammed the door. Jeez, the man thought it was her first day in the army. Everything about him irritated her.

I only have to work with him for two or three years. No big deal.

She stood in front of the car and held out her right arm to indicate that he should turn on that side's blinker. Then the left. She stalked around the back, consciously noting the tires looked inflated and didn't have worn treads, and repeated the exercise as Thane watched her in his rearview mirror. Right arm. Left arm. She'd never done this on a patrol car before, but over the years she'd done it on dozens of HUMM-Vs and a five-ton truck and—

She jumped a mile at an earsplitting burst of sirens. Blue and red lights flashed on top of the car, then stopped just as quickly. She swore, she swore, *she swore* that not only could she see Thane's shoulders shake with laughter, but she could hear the man laughing through the windows and over the sound of the car's engine.

She got back in and slammed the door. "Har-dee-har-har. You made the new guy jump."

"Yes, I did, Michaels."

They were going to use last names? Fine by her. She kept up her frosty pose as he powered up the laptop that was locked into place on a bracket between their seats. Thane hit a square on the touch screen to notify the dispatcher that 310 was now in service.

Chloe fastened her seat belt. Her handcuffs were situated on the back of her black belt in a bad spot. They were pressing into her spine, and the seatback pressed her weapon forward so that the muzzle end of the holster jabbed her in the thigh, but she'd be damned if she was going to wriggle all around to get comfy like a child. Like a new guy. A rookie.

Even if he was a first lieutenant and she only a second, lieutenants were generally considered one rank. They didn't salute each other. They called one another by their first names, but since Thane had just called her *Michaels*…

"It's going to be a long night, *Carter*." The last-name thing was good. Carter was whom she had to deal with. Thane could be a distant memory of a sucker's dream.

"Oh, it's going to be a long day, too, Michaels. A lot of long days." His smile was as mocking as his tone of voice as he put the car in Reverse and backed out of the parking lot. "In the morning, you're moving into my office."

Nothing happened on a Sunday, until it did.

It was nearly midnight, and Chloe and *Carter* were fixing themselves foam cups of coffee at the PX's Shoppette, a 24-hour convenience store on post. They stood on opposite sides of an island that held pots of hot coffee and all the accompaniments that went with them. They'd both chosen the brew labeled "Bold." Chloe was putting plain creamers in hers. On his side of the green Formica counter, Thane was adding all kinds of crazy crap to his cup. Cinnamon, vanilla powder, cocoa powder—every coffee garnish there was.

He had to be screwing with her, mocking her hot dog analysis. She pretended she wasn't watching.

They were the only two customers in the place, if they could be called customers. MPs got free coffee here all night long. Thane had turned down the volume on his radio, but the indistinct voice of the dispatcher rumbling from the little speaker clipped to his shoulder still overrode the overhead Muzak every few minutes.

Thane put one pump of vanilla syrup in his coffee. One pump of chocolate. One pump of caramel. One pump of sugar-free caramel—yep, he was screwing with her. She debated whether or not to tell him he was neither interesting nor amusing when he suddenly chucked the whole cup in the trash and started striding toward the door.

"Let's go, Michaels. That's us."

"What's us?"

Thane was already slamming the glass door open. This was not a drill. Chloe chucked her cup in the trash, too, and ran after him, calling a one-word apology to the store clerk as she burst out the door after Thane.

He was already in the car, engine on. She got in her side and had barely gotten her door closed before he backed out of the parking space. He hit the buttons for the lights and sirens—they weren't nearly as loud in the car as they were outside. Still, she reached for the two-way radio to turn up the volume just as he hit the street and floored the gas.

"Seat belt. Now. You check my right at intersections."

She complied with the seat belt. She guessed she was supposed to look right for oncoming traffic. Salvatore hadn't gone anywhere while using lights and sirens on Friday night, so she wasn't positive. So much for Sundays being slow.

"Where are we going?"

"Am I clear on the right?"

They'd already reached the next intersection. The light was red, but they were going through the intersection, anyway. "Yes. Clear."

But Thane had already bent forward to look around her head as he drove through the intersection.

She tried again. "What are we—"

"You call out 'clear on the right' or 'not clear.' Make sure that 'not clear' is loud."

"Roger. What's going on?"

"Officer down."

The radio chatter was nonstop now. Chloe picked out more words. "Domestic disturbance?"

"Shh." He shushed her angrily, listening to the radio and concentrating on the road as he sped toward whatever was causing nonstop radio chatter.

She shushed. A car ahead of them took an eternity to pull off the road and get out of their way. How could that driver not see red and blue lights flashing in the dark of the night?

The traffic light at the next intersection was red. "Clear on the right."

Thane slowed down, anyway.

"Clear on the right," she repeated. Did he not trust her? But no, out of the corner of her eye she saw he was concentrating on the left, wanting to be sure an oncoming car had seen their lights and was slowing down. He never even looked her way to see if the right was clear, since she'd said it was. He relied on her, as he should.

As they sped through the intersection, a male voice came on the radio, hard to understand because he was panting. "Hood, three-twenty, I'm up. I'm okay, suspect ran back in the house, blue shirt, basketball shorts."

Thane relaxed the tiniest bit.

Another radio voice said, "Three-thirty, out at three-twenty."

Thane turned off the main post road into one of the housing developments. He turned off the siren but left the emergency lights on. They were getting close, and Chloe needed to know what they were getting close to. The cuffs at her back and the holster on her thigh weren't toys. "You gotta clue me in."

"Domestic. That was three-twenty, the one out of breath.

He got into a wrestling match on the ground with a male. He's okay now, but the male got away and locked himself back in the house."

"With whomever called 911?"

"Gotta assume so. Three-thirty's there now for backup, but we're still going, too."

This was serious. The suspect had already attacked an MP. He could be in the house hurting his victim. He could be in the house arming himself with a personally owned weapon.

Thane killed the lights—not just the red and blue ones, but the headlights, as well.

Chloe had never felt more awake in her life, her brain and body both alert to real danger. "What's the address?"

"There." Thane rolled slowly past a street where another patrol car was parked with its emergency lights flashing in the night. He kept rolling along the side of the house on the corner, then braked. Waited.

Chloe looked where he was looking. The house on the corner was completely dark. Nobody home. "This corner house?"

"Yeah." He leaned forward a little farther. Without taking his eyes off the night, he put the car in Park, slowly. Undid his seat belt. Waited.

Chloe undid her seat belt.

"Look at the back porch," Thane said. "Do you see…?"

They'd gone dark and were on the side of the dark house. She couldn't see much of the back porch, only a corner of a patio awning and a few bushes.

A bush rustled.

"There he is." Thane exploded out of the car and started running.

Goddamn it, goddamn it—Chloe threw open her car door, feeling like she was moving in molasses, like one second was too long to take to get out of a car. She took off after Thane, but he shouted at her, "Call it in."

She didn't have a damned radio. She kept running after him. *"Go call it in."*

He was the ranking officer. She had to follow orders, even if it went against every instinct to let him go after the bad guy alone. She changed direction, ran back to the patrol car, yanked open the driver's door and ducked her head in, trying to keep an eye on her partner as she yanked the car radio's microphone out of its clip. She pressed its key.

"Three-ten." Now she was the one out of breath. She released the key. There was only silence on the other end of the radio. Damn it—she'd said three-ten first, as if she was trying to reach three-ten. She was trying to reach the Fort Hood dispatcher. "*Hood*, three-ten."

"Go ahead." The dispatcher sounded skeptical, since a woman was saying three-ten when everyone knew Lieutenant Carter was on duty.

"Three-ten is chasing down that domestic suspect. The male. On foot. They're headed down…the cross street."

Damn it again. She didn't know where they were. She looked at the computer screen and found the domestic disturbance dispatch in a second, but the address given wasn't this side street.

"Street name?" the dispatcher asked.

"Hold." She had to drop the mic and go halfway across the street to read the sign in the dark, run back and pick up the mic. "Bundy Street. Headed…" Crap. Was this street running north-south or east-west? She didn't know—but they'd been heading toward the airfield when they'd pulled off the main road, and they hadn't changed directions in the housing development. "Headed toward the airfield."

"Roger, three-ten. All units be advised, suspect is on foot—"

Chloe dropped the mic and backed out of the car, ready to run after Thane. As much as it was ingrained in her to obey lawful orders, it was also ingrained in her to never leave a team member to go it alone in combat. But she paused before slamming the door and joining the chase on foot. Logic ruled: minutes had passed since the chase had started. She'd never catch up.

She got back in the car and started the engine, then drove along the fence line. One of the other MPs, either 320 or 330, was running through the backyard now, too. He made a hard turn and headed down the backside of the block of houses, so the suspect must be running through yard after yard with Thane on his tail.

The suspect would have to come out at the end of the row of houses and cross another street. Chloe hit the gas. She could pass the MPs on foot and head the bad guy off the next street over. She looked in between every house, hoping for a glimpse of any of the three who were on foot. No luck— but just as she turned the corner, a man in a blue T-shirt and basketball shorts burst out of a backyard to cross the road.

She was right there in her marked police car, slamming on the brakes. The suspect stopped and changed direction to run from her car, but that sent him running right back toward Thane just as he burst out of the hedges and onto the street. Thane grabbed the suspect by one arm when he tried to dodge him, twisting it up behind the man as he resisted. Both men fell forward to the ground.

Chloe threw the car in Park and got out, running in the light of the headlights toward the two on the ground. Thane had the suspect down face-first and had control of one of the suspect's arms behind his back, but he couldn't get a handcuff on him because the suspect was flailing around with the other hand, awkwardly trying to reach behind himself blindly to hit at Thane.

Chloe started to grab for the suspect's flailing wrist, but saw the flash of a knife in the man's hand. She reared back from the blade and stepped on his forearm with her combat boot instead. "Drop the knife."

He didn't, but he was immobilized, so she knelt while keeping his forearm under her boot and started to pry his fingers from the knife, a kitchen knife by the looks of it. The guy was completely freaking out, using all his might to clutch the knife despite the fact that he was lying in the grass at the side of the road with two people pinning him down.

Thane was breathing hard and not talking. He closed one handcuff around the wrist he controlled. Chloe placed the palm of her hand on the suspect's shoulder. She spoke firmly. "This is over, soldier. This part is over. You know that. Let go of the knife so we can get you back on your feet and move on. This part is over."

The suspect was straining, holding his head up, but Chloe kept repeating herself. The suspect was under their control, his knife hand rendered useless. She didn't see a need to use any additional force. The suspect would tire on his own; he couldn't keep straining against them forever.

"Open your hand," she ordered, as calmly as she'd say *pass the ketchup.* "Let go of the knife. I can't hear your side of the story until we get these cuffs on."

With a wordless shout of despair and defeat, the suspect dropped his forehead into the scrubby grass and gave up, his muscles going slack, his hand opening and the knife falling out. Thane grabbed his wrist and jerked his arm out from under Chloe's boot before she could get off. She stood and kicked the knife to the middle of the road as Thane finished cuffing the suspect.

Another MP had come out from the backyards—either 320 or 330, Chloe assumed—and now bent forward to rest his hands on his knees and catch his breath. Thane stood up and dusted himself off. His breathing had nearly returned to normal. He lifted a hand to acknowledge the other MP, then wiped the side of his face on his jacket sleeve.

"Well, that was fun," he said.

Chloe knew that kind of army humor. When they were in the middle of an eight-hour road march that utterly sucked and the skies decided to open up and drench everyone, one soldier might conversationally say to the next, *Well, isn't that rain refreshing?* or *Great, I was hoping the road would turn to mud.*

So Chloe just shook her head. "Nothing happens on Sunday night, huh?"

"Didn't want you to get bored." Thane looked down at the suspect. "Let's get him to his feet."

They each took an arm and hauled him up, then walked him to the cruiser. As Thane patted him down, Chloe retrieved the knife, her first piece of evidence, ever. Once Thane had seated the suspect in the back seat and Chloe had popped the trunk to get out a proper plastic bag for the knife, they stood once more on opposite sides of the patrol car. Over the roof, Thane asked, "Are you ready for some more fun?"

"Like what?"

"Now you get to hear his side of the story."

Chapter Eight

It wasn't that fun.

The suspect's side of the story consisted mostly of four-letter words. He cursed Michaels almost exclusively, although Thane was the one who'd caught him.

Thane told himself that it was just part of the job. He told himself that Michaels needed to get a thick skin and get it fast if she was going to spend years as an MP. He told himself that he'd heard worse said about himself. He'd heard worse said to other female MPs. He'd heard—

"I thought you were going to tell us your side of the story?" Thane interrupted. "All we're getting is some piss-poor attempt to impress us with your vocabulary."

The suspect paused in his tirade to throw a few curses Thane's way, then resumed calling Michaels every name in the book. Thane guessed that she was a bigger threat to the loser's manhood than he was. The suspect could tell his buddies that a man had chased him down without losing face. Clearly, he had an issue with a woman rendering his arm immobile and his knife useless. After all, this particular suspect had been beating a helpless woman. He wouldn't want a woman to be able to fight back.

Fortunately, it took only a minute to get back to the suspect's house. An ambulance had arrived, contributing its emergency lights to the patrol cars of 320 and 330.

They left the suspect in the back seat with both his seat belt and handcuffs on and headed up the walkway toward the house. Thane caught Michaels squinting away from the flashing emergency lights. If one were prone to migraines or seizures, the lights would be crippling, really. He didn't have to worry about that with Michaels, however. He was certain Michaels was as healthy as all get-out, because...

He pushed away the memory of Chloe in a bikini.

Because Michaels wouldn't have been commissioned if she had epilepsy. *That* was why he was certain.

But the lights could be painful to anyone's eyes, so as they passed 320's patrol car, Thane opened the driver's door and reached in to shut off the emergency lights. Same with the next car. He didn't touch the ambulance. He wasn't responsible for that vehicle, and the paramedics were going to be running with lights to get the victim to the hospital, judging from the chatter on his radio…radio chatter that Michaels probably couldn't hear, standing an arm's distance away from him. He probably should have listened to her and let her draw a radio.

He placed his hand over the speaker clipped to his shoulder. "They're going to take the wife to the hospital."

"How do you know…?" She looked at his hand. "Never mind."

Thane hoped he was pulling off the stoic army officer face again. A trainee didn't need a radio. She'd said that Salvatore hadn't given her one on Friday, either. Thane wasn't going to feel guilty about it. "The other MPs are in the house with the paramedics. It gets crowded. I'm waiting out here, because there's no reason to wade in there and have the MPs feeling obliged to stop and report to us. Plus, we've got that bozo in our back seat."

Michaels had her arms crossed over her chest as she stood on the street beside him, facing the front door of the house. She had that fierce look on her face again, that one that meant she was concentrating on something critical.

Thane looked around. The situation was under control. There weren't even any nosy neighbors to herd away. He wondered what she was concentrating on. After hearing the suspect's F-word-laden side of the story, Thane could guess.

"Don't put too much stock into the suspect's ranting. You'll hear worse, you know. I've been called every name in the book by now."

Her gaze ricocheted from the house to him. "I'm a big girl. I can handle cursing."

Her dark eyes reflected the ambulance lights. Her voice was steady. She didn't seem to be shaken up at all by the chase or by facing her first armed suspect. He felt proud of her—no, that was ridiculous. He was just glad she seemed to be able to handle herself because she was going to be part of his company. He was relieved that he wouldn't have to coddle a thin-skinned butter bar, that was all. She was taking this in stride.

He approved.

Meanwhile, Michaels shrugged. "You can almost feel sorry for him. He's the most miserable human being I've ever seen, really, almost like a wild thing, lashing out at anyone he can see. He's lost everything, and he knows it. I'm sure he'll be court-martialed and kicked out of the service. There goes his salary. There goes his house. There goes his life. It's all his own fault. He's made himself powerless."

Thane was silent. Her level of understanding, even her sense of compassion, struck him as extraordinary for someone so new to it all. He looked at Chloe's profile, at beauty illuminated by flashes of red and white against a black night, and felt that kick in his chest again, that loss of knowing he'd never be able to have this woman in his life.

Keep it in check, Thane.

He did have her in his life, as a fellow platoon leader. It was good from a professional standpoint that she hadn't taken the suspect's ranting personally. It was interesting, nothing more, to hear her thoughts on the suspect and how he was lashing out because his life as he knew it was over.

How long would that compassion last? This was only her second night in the real world.

There was a commotion at the front door of the house. A paramedic, his back to them, pulled one end of a stretcher through the front door. A woman was propped up on the stretcher. Beside Thane, Michaels's expression remained neutral, as did his own, but the victim's expression was undeniably heartbreaking. There was all the sorrow, there was the misery that had been missing in the suspect's rant.

The paramedics had put one of the victim's arms in a sling. With the other, she clutched a towel to her head, a white towel soaked in red blood, vivid in the red and white ambulance lights.

Michaels took in a single deep breath, then turned around and walked back to the patrol car.

Maybe she was hiding her shock at the extent of the injuries. Maybe she was hiding tears. She'd handled the chase, the apprehension, even the suspect's insults just fine, but seeing a helpless victim, that must be Michaels's weakness.

Thane couldn't blame her. The injured woman looked so small on the stretcher, so much smaller than the man who was locked in his back seat. It infuriated Thane that a man could even think about using fists and knives against a person so defenseless.

"Carter," Michaels called. She didn't sound weak. She didn't sound shaken.

Thane turned around.

She was standing at their patrol car, directly in front of the window where the suspect sat. "Come here and help me block his view of her. He shouldn't get to gloat over his handiwork, the bastard. God knows she shouldn't have to see his face right now."

So maybe Michaels wasn't weak or tearful at the sight of the victim. Maybe she was pissed and protective. A good combo. She had great potential. Great instincts. His first impression of her, that she was something special…

Forget that first poolside impression.

Thane stood beside her and helped her block the victim's view of her attacker. Through the closed car, the suspect's voice was muffled as he ranted at the world some more. Thane paid as little attention to it as Michaels did.

She watched the paramedics loading their patient into the ambulance. "What's next?"

"Now, we get to enjoy the beauty of being three-ten." Thane crossed his arms over his black vest and leaned against the patrol car. He could feel the suspect kicking the door, a little thunk of vibration against Thane's back. "We're going to put this wonderful human being in three-twenty's car. This is his case. He gets to transport the suspect to the holding cell at the station and handle the paperwork. You and I will get back on the road and wait for the next call."

As the duty officer, he was required to go to all felonies and domestic disturbances. Other than that, 310 basically served as backup to the entire post, rolling by when they were near a call, checking on every MP who was out there at least once during the shift. They could go to any call that sounded interesting, a perk of being the duty officer instead of a regular patrol confined to one smaller area of post. There had to be some perk for these thirty-six-hour shifts.

"If there is another call, that is. Sundays really are boring."

Chloe could feel Thane staring at her as he sat behind the steering wheel, buckling his seat belt.

She glared back.

Thane put the car in gear and headed out of the housing development. "Let's go back to the Shoppette and get that coffee."

Chloe pushed her seat belt lower across her lap, under her belt full of equipment that she hadn't used. There was only one item she'd needed at the scene. "I don't need coffee. I need a damned radio."

"Look, you did really well. Using the car to cut off his route was a great idea. I don't know what all your pissed-off-ness is for. You did fine."

"The reason I had to drive the car was because you ordered me to stay behind to use a radio that was attached to the car. You ran after him alone and put yourself at risk. What if I hadn't gotten there?"

"Then I would have taken him on my own."

"He had a knife."

"I'm aware of that. You don't always get a partner, Michaels. If you weren't there, I would have dealt with it. You better be able to handle things solo, too."

"This isn't about me being solo on some future hypothetical call. It's about you failing to use your resources wisely. I am your resource tonight, but you wasted me on a radio call." She waited for him to tell her she had a lot of nerve, calling herself a resource when she was the new kid on the block.

He didn't say that. "I didn't waste the fact that I had an extra person with me. Someone had to call it in."

"*Someone* could have made the call as she ran, if she'd had a handheld radio. You set me up for failure, and in this case, that could have been deadly. For you."

"I set you up for failure? Failure?"

"You asked me to do something you knew I couldn't do. I didn't have a radio and I didn't know what to say. I told you I'm barely catching all the call signs, and you didn't even tell me which street we were on. I looked like an idiot. Or I sounded like an idiot."

"I doubt that."

"What is the code for 'officer running on foot after the suspect'? I didn't know. What if it had gone differently and you were the one who got tackled? What is the code for 'officer down'?"

"You can just say 'officer down.' We're discouraging codes. They don't mean the same thing from one town to the next. Use plain language."

"Really? And what was said on your radio that made you chuck your coffee and run?"

He hesitated. She saw his jaw clench. "Nine-nine-nine."

"Which means?"

"Officer down."

She threw up her hands. "Point proven. I wouldn't have known to say nine-nine-nine if I'd gone into those bushes and found that you were the one who was pinned down. While you were trying to teach me a little lesson on how unprepared I am for this job, you put yourself in danger."

"Teach you a little lesson? You think I was intentionally trying to make you look bad?"

"Yes."

There was a moment of silence on Thane's part as they sat at a red light. Then he started shaking his head slowly. "In the middle of witnessing a suspect fleeing the scene, I stopped and thought to myself, 'Hey, how can I make Michaels look bad? I know, I'll make her call it in to the station when she doesn't know how.'"

Her mistakes had been broadcast to every MP working tonight, to the dispatchers and to the watch commander. Chloe's first impression on the people she was required to lead wasn't going to be good, and she knew it would be hard to overcome. She had Carter to thank for it, as if he hadn't already gone low enough yesterday by pretending to be attracted to her when he didn't even like her face.

"Why *wouldn't* I think that? You've already—" She wasn't going to mention the pool. The flashlight incident would do. "You've already tried to make me look bad with your little flashlight stunt."

He shrugged, completely unconcerned. "I'm sure you did fine on the radio. I didn't give you a task I didn't think you could handle. You're the one who gave yourself the task with the flashlights."

She didn't want to go off on a tangent about flashlights. *Controlled confrontation.* "I need a radio before we do anything else tonight."

"I was already planning to stop at the station to get you one. I was going to get you a cup of coffee first. Forget it. We'll just go to the station."

"Good."

It was hard to believe that just yesterday afternoon she'd been eager to eat an entire dinner with this man. Now, even a cup of coffee would taste sour if he was around.

Chapter Nine

Second Lieutenant Chloe Michaels was done being a badass—at least for the next twelve hours.

She was almost home. Her apartment building was visible through her windshield. She parked her Charger and got out, putting on her patrol cap and pulling the brim down just so. She forced herself to put one foot in front of the other, trudging past the swimming pool without one glance toward the blue water…or the little table for two.

Man, she was tired. It hadn't even been thirty-six hours, just twenty-four since she'd reported for duty at the police station. She'd never admit it to a soul at the 584th, but twenty-four hours was a very long time to stay sharp and act her best among strangers in a strange place. She'd tried to make a positive first impression while mentally filing away her first impressions of everyone she met—which had seemed to be nearly every soldier out of the one hundred and twenty in her company. She was grateful that literally every soldier in the US Army wore a name tag.

Chloe passed the mailboxes without stopping, since she didn't care if there was a flyer posted for another poolside event coming up. She already had a close friend, thank you very much. As soon as she got to her apartment, she'd check in with Different Drummer. She'd been away from her laptop for so long, and she missed him. He already knew her; she already knew him. She could slouch on the couch and talk about *Star Trek* or Scottish poets, and Drummer wouldn't be shocked or appalled or even impressed by the new lieutenant in the unit. He'd just laugh with Ballerina Baby.

She started up the concrete stairs. At least she felt reasonably confident that she'd made it through the last twenty-four hours without shocking or appalling anyone, except maybe Lieutenant Carter. The night had been one long, unrelenting trial of having to deal with Carter, but the day had gone better.

For one thing, she had a platoon sergeant who seemed to know what he was doing. Sergeant First Class Ernesto had decided she needed a tour of her new world, and she'd been relieved to have him escort her to the barracks, to the motor pool, to the dining facility.

She'd needed that break from Tha—Carter. Except for the minutes she'd spent in the bathroom, she'd been with him for every single second of each of the twelve hours in the patrol car. Even the bathroom hadn't been much of a break; she couldn't help looking in the mirror and wondering what was wrong with her face.

Worse, Carter hadn't been kidding about sharing an office with him. Little wonder that she'd jumped at the chance to go to the motor pool with her new platoon sergeant.

The same office. *The same office.*

She'd get through it. She had no choice but to get through it. Chloe slogged her way to the second-story landing and paused for a deep breath. Why had she chosen an apartment on the third floor? One more flight. Then she could collapse.

At least her platoon sergeant had gotten a good impression of her before she'd even walked into the headquarters building. *Nice to meet you, ma'am*, had been followed immediately by *Word is, you had quite the night.*

She'd held her breath as her platoon sergeant had told her what he'd heard. She knew he hadn't heard anything from Carter, because she'd been with Carter. But whomever he'd heard it from, it was all good. Three-thirty must have seen her kneeling over the suspect, immobilizing his arm with her boot. He'd seen her kick the knife out of the way. She was particularly relieved to hear that, despite feeling like an idiot on the radio, she'd apparently come across as calm and collected when her voice had been broadcasted to every MP on post.

The accuracy of the platoon sergeant's intel impressed

her. "Is all of this gossip, or did this come out on an official report somewhere?"

"Gossip, ma'am?" Sergeant First Class Ernesto had pretended horror, making her smile as they walked down the line of their HUMM-Vs. "We're all members of the United States Army here. We don't have time to gossip."

"Sure, you don't."

"But word can travel around here at combat speed. When the word involved the new LT, that invisible hotline between our building and the station just about burned up."

"In that case, thank God that hotline had a good report on me. I'll take it."

Chloe reached the last step of her climb. The third-story landing could have been made of gold instead of concrete, she was so glad to see it. She unlocked her door, walked into the cold air-conditioning and stood there. She took her patrol cap off automatically, but she was too tired to remember what she was supposed to do next. In the dark apartment, the sky looked bright beyond the sliding glass doors to her balcony. The first colorful clouds of the approaching sunset were visible between the two buildings on the other side of the complex. Now she remembered: that balcony, that view, that was why she'd wanted the third floor.

She sank onto her new, red couch. She ought to pour herself a glass of wine and drink it on the balcony…but she made no move toward the kitchen. First, she unlaced her boots and hauled each one off with one hand. She looked toward the kitchen. She looked out the sliding glass door. And then she turned and did a face-plant on her couch, which felt as welcoming as a bed of red roses.

She slept.

Thane bunched the pillow under his head and tried not to be absurdly emotional about his pen pal.

Ballerina was gone.

Since the discussion they'd had after their failed friend-experiment on Saturday, she hadn't posted anything. Not one hello, not one silly sentence.

He missed her. He'd been looking forward to talking tonight with a woman who didn't annoy the hell out of him.

He'd been stuck for a solid twenty-four hours in the Chloe Michaels show. The entire company was buzzing with positive crap about everything she did. Soldiers were bound to like an officer who wasn't afraid to jump in during a physical altercation, but even the stupid stuff was working in her favor. The ludicrously formal way she'd conducted her inspection had somehow fulfilled everyone's expectations of how a West Pointer ought to render military courtesies, as if his soldiers had forgotten that there were other West Point officers of various ranks already in the battalion, including the commander of the 410th, the operations officer on battalion staff—hell, Thane didn't keep track of everyone's commissioning source, but there were more. The point was, Michaels was far from the first one anyone had ever met.

But she was the newest. And she was female, which shouldn't matter, but it did. Add in her good looks and the way she seemed equally comfortable talking to the most junior private or the battalion commander, and—well, she was a novelty, that was all. Thane just had to grit his teeth until the buzz died down.

Between that eternally long ride-along and the steady stream of curious folks who'd come by his office all day, he'd only had a couple minutes of privacy to check his phone. Each time, the app's white screen had been frustratingly blank. Nothing pink to pick him up.

Now that he was home, he'd spent the last two hours trying to reach Ballerina.

Nothing.

The last time they'd talked, he'd given her advice, encouraging her to confront her adversary, but now he realized he hadn't really had enough information. After the domestic he'd worked last night, he was worried. The image of the wife on the stretcher, bloody towel to her head, wouldn't go away. She'd looked so frail compared to the man Thane had apprehended.

Thane stared at the empty phone screen and wondered what Ballerina's physical appearance was like. Was she frail? She worked out, he knew that, but if she was a wisp of a ballet dancer, should she really be confronting adversaries?

She'd been upset by a man. She'd told him the friend-who-wasn't-a-friend was male. What if she got hurt?

The thought made his stomach turn, made every muscle in his body tense. Where was she?

Hey, Ballerina Baby.

His cursor blinked for long minutes.

He'd been at work for only twenty-four hours, not thirty-six, so he wasn't as tired as usual. Thane adjusted the pillow one more time and settled in to write her a letter.

It's been two days, but it feels like a week since I last talked to you. You are never far from my thoughts.

That had been true once he'd gotten rid of Michaels. The moment her platoon sergeant had taken her off to the motor pool, Thane had checked this app. Before that, it had been all Michaels, all of the time—not all of it bad. He could still see the look on her face when she'd stood in front of the patrol car window, so that a victim wouldn't have to see her abuser. Pissed off and protective, he'd thought at the time. Who would protect Ballerina like that, if Thane's poor advice had caused her to be hurt?

I hope you haven't had any more run-ins with your friend that isn't really a friend. I wish you could give me more details, because my imagination is running wild. When I suggested confrontation, I didn't take into account that confrontations can turn physical. I'd only been thinking about speaking your mind, but this guy could be more dangerous than you think. If you have the tiniest bit of an unsettled feeling about him and his potential for violence, stay in public whenever he's around. Has he ever tried to get you alone? I regret advising you to confront him without insisting on more details first. I forget sometimes that women are vulnerable.

Probably because the women he worked with were MPs who were armed and trained. They'd stand on a man's arm or kick away his knife. But Ballerina? Thane might have advised her to confront a man who could be twice her size, for all he knew.

I wish I had some way to check on you when you go silent on this app. I worry about you, Ballerina. I'm afraid this new advice is too late. Please drop me a line when you see this, even if you don't have time for a long conversation. Heck, a single word will let me breathe easier. So please, Baby, check in.

Thane stared at his blue words a moment. No ironic quotes or movie references came to mind—just real worries. He set his phone on his nightstand. Whether he'd been up twenty-four hours or thirty-six, he needed to sleep. Tomorrow would be another long day at work, and he'd have to spend it with Michaels taking up space in his own office.

Was it just Friday night that he'd been feeling isolated, a man who slept and worked and did little else? Suddenly, women had taken center stage in his life, women like Chloe Michaels. Hard to believe he'd ever spent an entire afternoon smiling at her in the shade. She was beautiful and smart and too confident for her own good. She was going to be a thorn in his side.

Women like Ballerina Baby. He craved a conversation

with her, but she was missing and there was nothing he could do about it. God, he hoped she was safe.

Then there was the woman on the stretcher, a tragic image etched in his brain by flashes of red and white lights...

Thane punched his pillow into shape. One good thing about working for twenty-four hours: he'd be able to sleep even with all these women on his mind.

Eventually.

Thane had to punch his pillow into shape a few more times before sleep would come.

Chloe woke to the sound of a car engine, and another. And another.

They were muted by the sliding glass door, but the fact that there were so many must have permeated her consciousness enough to wake her up. She forced her eyes open and blinked at the gloom of her apartment. The dim sunlight outside her sliding glass door hadn't changed. It was still sunset.

The engine sounds faded in the distance. Where was everyone going? It was like an evacuation order had been given, an order she'd totally missed.

Orders. The army.

"Oh, crap." It hit her all at once. It wasn't sunset; it was sunrise. Sunrise in the army meant it was time for PT, or physical training. That meant calisthenics, the daily dozen, followed by group runs with cadences being called to keep everyone in step.

Here at the Two Rivers apartment complex, that meant half the residents were all leaving at the same time to get onto post before 6:30 a.m.—and it meant Chloe was late.

She ignored every sore muscle in her body, every stiff joint from sleeping on a sofa rather than her bed. She'd slept on worse, on dirt, branches, rocks. She'd slept sitting up in trenches she'd dug. This discomfort was nothing.

She stripped out of her ACUs, all the way to the skin, on her way to her bedroom. She pulled out the top drawer of her childhood dresser and grabbed some fresh underwear. She wrestled her way past the strong elastic of a clean sports bra, yanked open the second drawer and pulled out the black T-shirt of the army's physical fitness uniform. Jeez, she hadn't had a chance to shower since reporting to duty Sunday afternoon. It was Tuesday morning. She ran into her bathroom, threw on some deodorant and then her shirt.

In shirt and underpants, she brushed her teeth, then looked in the mirror—*screw you, Thane*—and fished all the bobby pins out of the remains of her bun, tossing them onto the hard counter, where they skittered off in all directions. With the elastic ponytail holder clamped in her teeth, she started ripping a brush through her hair. Fast.

Move, move, move, to be late is to be dead...

They'd killed her for lateness at West Point, that was for sure. Each simple tardy to class had resulted in four hours of walking the area in Dress Gray—with a rifle, of course, just to make the suck more of a suck—back and forth over a paved square that was surrounded on all sides by barracks buildings, in silent monotony, hour after hour. What kind of punishment was there in the regular army? What would the commander do to her?

He couldn't do anything that would be worse than the way she was blowing the positive first impression she'd made yesterday. Twenty-four hours of good work would go down the toilet when she came rushing up, panting and late, to the PT formation. Her whole platoon would know she'd failed to make it on time.

Her stomach hurt.

She was starving. Lunch yesterday had been a long, long time ago. That was okay. She'd done worse, gone for days without food during survival training. How far did the company run on a typical Tuesday? Two miles? Three? She could handle that without any fuel in her body.

She used her hands to pull her hair back into a ponytail, a style allowed only during PT. *Pants.* She bolted back to her bedroom dresser, yanked open the second dresser drawer, then paused. Was she supposed to wear the PT uniform's pants or shorts on this post? They'd been in pants at Leonard Wood, but it was so much warmer here. What had this post's commander authorized as the uniform? She jogged to her bedroom window and peeked through the blinds, hoping to spot someone else on their way to PT.

Half the cars in the parking lot were gone. The ones that had woken her had probably been the last few, doors slamming and engines revving, peeling out of here because they were running late. Even though only a couple of minutes had passed since she'd woken, there was no way she'd make it downstairs, drive to Hood, park at the headquarters building, run to the PT field and be standing in front of her platoon by six thirty.

She still had to go. Better late than never, she supposed. But she returned to the bathroom at a walk, not a run. She was thirsty. She could run three miles hungry, but not dehydrated. PT wasn't a life-or-death situation, but that kind of foolishness could turn it into one, or at least into something serious. She'd seen people pass out in run formations, hitting the pavement and getting trampled by the next row. Chloe filled her cup with tap water and chugged it down while watching herself in the mirror.

"This isn't life or death." She said it out loud to her reflection, sternly, because her heart was pounding as hard as if her whole world was on the line. She still felt like a cadet, trying to meet impossible demands: memorize the menus for the day, the front-page stories from the newspaper and all the other daily knowledge upperclassmen required, polish her shoes, shine her brass, prepare her room for inspection, ping—walk briskly—to an academic building to pass a multivariable calculus exam, then run back to the barracks to get into full regalia for an afternoon parade.

Her heart must have beat this hard more days than not, especially during plebe year. Panic had become a normal emotional state, one she'd learned to function well in. If Drummer were here, he'd say it was understandable that she was defaulting into that mind-set now, because that's what had worked in the past.

Perhaps that hadn't been the best thing to learn at her alma mater.

Chloe was in trouble for missing PT, of that she had no doubt, but what good did it serve to rush about in panic now? This was a new life. An adult life. A better thing her alma mater had taught her was to take ownership of her failures. Cadets could not say anything except *No excuse, sir* when asked why something had gone wrong or something had been left undone. It had rankled as an eighteen-year-old, wanting to explain all the circumstances but being able to say only those three words. Now, it was second nature.

She'd missed PT this morning. No excuse. This situation wasn't ideal, especially not on her second day in the unit, but she'd report to the commander, apologize for being late, and take whatever butt-chewing he dished out. She would stand through it without flinching—and *that*, her alma mater had certainly taught her how to do.

Then she'd sit in her new office, five feet from Thane Carter, for twelve hours.

Chloe stared at her reflection a moment longer. She told herself her stomach hurt because of hunger, not dread. She pulled off her black shirt and turned on the shower. She was going to report to the commander showered, fed, hydrated, wearing her ACUs and looking like the calm—not panicked—professional military officer she was.

And *then* she'd deal with Thane Carter for twelve hours.

Chapter Ten

Chloe used her extra time to stop at the drive-through doughnut shop on her way to the post. She bought a dozen doughnuts, all different flavors, plus one extra for herself. The doughnuts were a shameless attempt at damage control, a small positive after the big negative of oversleeping.

The headquarters building was nearly empty. PT had finished, and everyone had gone to their quarters to shower and eat and return in ACUs for the rest of their day. Chloe had time to kill. She savored her doughnut, wiped the sugar off her lips, shot the balled-up napkin for two points into the basket that was Thane's trash can, then turned her chair over to figure out which wheel was making that god-awful squeaking noise.

As soon as she heard her platoon sergeant arrive down the hall, she picked up the doughnut box and headed to his office. Even though she was his boss, she owed him an apology. Maybe *because* she was his boss, she needed to apologize for letting their whole platoon down. At the very least, she owed him the first pick of the doughnuts.

She told him the truth. She'd overslept. No excuse.

Ernesto seemed surprised. "The platoon wasn't at PT this morning, ma'am. During garrison duty, the soldiers working shifts are excused. It's pretty much just headquarters at PT."

Only headquarters did the routine 6:30 a.m. PT during garrison months? It made sense. The supply sergeant, the motor pool mechanics and the rest kept regular hours, but the MPs performing law enforcement did not. Her platoon hadn't been out there in the predawn, running in formation without her.

She didn't even try to keep the relief out of her voice. "I'm so glad to hear that. I'll just go explain to the CO, then."

"Well, ma'am, you can do that if you want to, but I don't

think it's necessary. You officers usually write where you're going on that whiteboard in the orderly room. When you weren't at PT this morning, I took the liberty of writing 'in-processing' next to your name. No one's expecting you to be at any particular formation today."

Chloe was speechless. He'd covered for her, and he'd done it in a perfectly reasonable way. For four years, she'd heard that every new lieutenant needed to pray for a good platoon sergeant, because a good one could smooth the way. She'd assumed that meant the sergeant would know all the right paperwork forms to use or how to procure the right equipment, but this? She wasn't in trouble. At all.

Ernesto prompted her. "You do still have some in-processing to take care of, right? You're authorized five days, and they had you riding along on at least one of those. Gotta get a parking pass or drop your medical records at the clinic or something?"

"Yes, of course. I'll go take care of…something like that today." Forget Thane Carter, forget Different Drummer—Sergeant First Class Ernesto was her favorite man in the world right now.

She handed him the entire box of doughnuts. "Could you find a home for these, please?"

He took them with a smile. "Roger that, ma'am."

Chloe smiled, too, all the way back to her own office, practically dizzy with relief, until she saw that Carter had arrived. He was at his desk, typing something on his personal phone, scowling away, and he didn't even greet her with a grunt.

She sat in her chair. The wheels squeaked loudly. There was no way he didn't know she'd walked in.

"Good morning," she said, just because Carter didn't want to talk.

He tossed his phone onto his desk, but didn't stop scowling.

"Bad news?" she asked, nodding toward his phone.

"No news." His scowl didn't let up. "Why does it smell like doughnuts in here?"

"I don't know." She shrugged and did the first thing that would make her look busy—opening her government-issued laptop. Her personal laptop was still sitting in her apartment, as it should be, but she wished she could write to Drummer. She'd ask him if he'd ever dreaded something he'd been sure would be hell, but then it had turned out to be a piece of cake? Or a doughnut? That was it—she could make him laugh by telling him that she'd had nothing but a box of doughnuts with which to face a hellish morning, but a coworker had turned her morning into a piece of cake. She'd taken the cake and given away the doughnuts, and gotten the better end of the bargain.

She stared at the army laptop's unfunny home screen. It felt like a million years since she'd last talked to Drummer. It would be at least another ten hours before she got home. Meanwhile, she only had Carter to talk to, a handsome man who hated her, a man who was raising an eyebrow at her in question.

Oops—she'd been looking at him instead of her screen.

"You're riding along with me again tomorrow night." Carter looked about as thrilled as she felt.

"Great," she said with zero enthusiasm. The more he glared at her, the more she craved the warmth and approval she got from Drummer.

Tonight. She just had to wait until the flag was lowered tonight, and then she could leave Carter's hostile company and go spend the evening with Drummer.

He was such a better man.

Dear Drummer,

I just got home and read your letter. I'm so sorry you've been so worried. Nothing terrible happened to me. I was away from my laptop, and couldn't check our app. I've been missing you!

Chloe hit Send on that much and stopped to unlace her boots and take off her jacket. She was determined not to pass out tonight before doing the essential things, like eating dinner, and most of all, talking to Drummer.

Drummer came first, food could come second. The emotional blue words he'd written had tugged at her heartstrings. How wonderful it was to have someone really worry for her. How awful it was that she'd given him cause to worry.

The only terrible thing that happened was that I made you worry for no reason. I'm so sorry. I didn't forget you. I just wasn't physically near my laptop. You were always on my mind.

She pulled off her socks and wiggled her bare toes. She could feel Second Lieutenant Michaels giving way, relaxing, morphing into Chloe, lover of the ballet and pop culture and Scottish poetry, lover of Drummer's words and thoughts and friendship, just a girl in love with her boyfriend.

Just a virtual boyfriend—but he was a real person. But not a man she knew in real life.

Thane Carter was a man in real life. Annoyingly, an image of him popped into her mind. Not Carter the MP officer, sweating from a foot chase, cuffing a suspect. Not the fellow platoon leader kicking back in his desk chair, smirking at her. For just a brief moment, she remembered the Thane Carter who'd knelt beside her at the edge of the pool, offering her a beer and a towel and his company. The sun had been shining and the water had been blue...

Well, that had gone nowhere.

Drummer was so much better. He didn't insult her face, for starters. He hadn't ever seen her face, but if he did, she was sure he wouldn't hate it. He surely would never stand around with other guys in public and discuss her shortcomings.

She carried the laptop into the kitchen. Blue letters suddenly ripped across the screen. There you are!!!! Thank God. Where have you been? Who were you with? Not the jerk I told you to confront, I hope.

Oh, boy. Drummer was real, all right. Real and upset. She set the laptop down next to the fridge, but she didn't type immediately. If she decided the jerk he referred to was Keith from her cadet days, then she could say she hadn't run into him again yet. But really, the jerk they'd discussed Saturday night was Thane, whom she had confronted and now had to work with.

Drummer wrote into her silence. I'm sorry. I'm not trying to interrogate you. The only truly important question is this: Are you safe?

She'd already said that she was okay. What made Drummer suddenly afraid she might come to physical harm? She'd been obsessed with keeping her heart safe, not her actual body. Yet Drummer was worried enough that he'd missed her Willie Nelson quote, *You were always on my mind*.

She hadn't meant to scare him with her neglect. The guilt she felt for taking their virtual relationship for granted felt very real.

More blue words filled the silence. (Willie Nelson, by the way. Too easy.)

I'm physically safe, I promise. Safe and so relieved he was still teasing her with a *too easy*.

Chloe blew a kiss at her screen and opened the fridge. Yogurt and coffee creamer and some leftover macaroni and cheese huddled together on one shelf in the otherwise-empty fridge. She put the mac and cheese in the microwave and got a spoon to start on the yogurt. She could eat and type.

Emotionally, I'm doing all right, too, now that I'm getting to take a break and catch up with you. If my goal in Big Life is happiness, then I need to talk to you as often as possible. It makes me happy. (Could be Elvis, too, you know. He sang it first.)

Her pink words hadn't pushed all his blue words off the bottom of the screen yet. She reread them. He sounded so different. Something had happened to Drummer. She was almost certain.

What makes you think I could be in physical danger? she asked.

Bad things happen to good people.

She abandoned the spoon in the yogurt and ignored the beeping of the microwave. What happened to you? Are YOU safe?

I'm fine. Wasn't talking about myself. I just saw some things at work that

The words just ended. Chloe shifted from bare foot to bare foot on the cold linoleum as she waited.

This anonymity thing has its limitations, he wrote. I can't tell you about my job and you can't tell me about yours. But can you tell me if you are safe at work? Safe at home?

Chloe went still. At work, she carried a loaded Beretta and drove at high rates of speed through red lights. Was she safe?

She remembered Thane's drop-everything response to the nine-nine-nine code, the way 330 had arrived so quickly to assist. Two more patrols had been on their way before dispatch called them off once 320 had radioed that he was safe.

I stay very safe at work. I am never alone. I always have reliable colleagues around me.

Including Thane. He'd been so callous and careless with

her heart, but if she ever said nine-nine-nine into a radio, he'd do whatever it took to get to her.

She'd do the same for him.

It was an unquestionable commitment that was hard to explain to civilians. For Drummer, she tried. I honestly feel safer at work than I would if I were out on the town by myself.

I'm glad to hear it. You have no idea how glad. Maybe we should rethink that confrontation plan tonight, though. Even someone you think would never hurt you might.

Too late. I already had it out with him.

God. And you're ok. Good. How did he take it?

He took it like a man. Chloe deleted that as soon as she wrote it. It sounded too much like a positive trait. He didn't run away. That's something. She hit Send.

Did he apologize?

No. But he didn't try to gaslight me, either, and pretend I was remembering things wrong. He didn't play like it was no big deal or say he'd just been kidding and I was over-reacting. I hate when people do that.

Years of living with *No excuse, sir* had made her pretty intolerant of excuses, she supposed. She did have to work with Thane, so it was good to know he wasn't the kind to make up excuses. Too bad he was the kind who tried to charm a woman he wasn't really interested in, just for kicks, just for an ego boost.

If I'd done the usual avoid-conflict thing, then I would have been the one playing it off like it was no big deal, which would probably have already resulted in me giving myself an ulcer overnight. Laying everything out plainly was good. I wouldn't say it made me happy, but at least I don't feel like a doormat right now.

From there, Chloe and Drummer eased into their comfortable relationship and spent the evening cracking jokes about leftover food and the remains of a television series that should have ended at least one season earlier than they did.

She couldn't ignore her hunch, though, that some aspect of Drummer's life made him think women were vulnerable. She knew he wasn't a billionaire and there was no reason to assume he was a drummer any more than she was a ballerina, but with his knowledge of Thoreau and Shakespeare, she'd always pictured him in an erudite kind of profession. If he was a drummer, then he was a percussionist in a symphony, perhaps, or a man seeking a PhD in music studies.

She had to frame it a little differently now. He must be around a grittier way of life. Maybe he was the drummer in a rock band, a big star who'd seen too many women crushed by crowds or overdosing on drugs at wild backstage parties.

Okay, that was a bit far-fetched. More realistically, he'd be the drummer in a fledgling rock band that was playing gigs until closing time in bars that had back alleys. Dangerous back alleys. Had he seen a woman become the victim of a terrible crime?

She was so very tempted to suggest they reveal their professions. He might be reassured to know she was a soldier and an MP.

Or not.

He might worry even more. Most people thought of the military as a dangerous profession. Law enforcement was considered a dangerous profession. Put them both together…

He wouldn't feel better at all.

She couldn't change their relationship and make the man feel worse at the same time.

The best leftover in the world is fried chicken. **She hit Send with a sigh.**

No way. The coating gets all soggy in the microwave. If you can't nuke it, it's not a good leftover.

Chloe rolled her eyes. **He was such a dude sometimes.** You don't microwave it. You eat it ice-cold, preferably while standing in front of an open refrigerator door.

You're weird.

Do you know what else tastes great, no matter how long it's been left out?

I'm afraid of this answer.

Candy, candy canes, candy corn and syrup. **Chloe hit Send, and waited. One second, two—**

Elf—great Christmas movie. (And too easy.)

There. She'd made Drummer feel better. Telling him she was an MP in the US Army would only have made him feel worse.

It wouldn't have made her feel good, either, to be honest. Once people found out where she'd gone to school or that she was an officer, they expected her to act a certain way, all gung-ho and oo-rah. Her career was a huge part of her life, but it wasn't every minute of it. The last time she'd been home, she'd gone to her mother's book club's tea party. She'd been having fun, until she was asked what she did for a living. Once her profession was known, there'd been the inevitable questions, even requests for demonstrations, like could she do a man's push-up?

Duh. As if there were even such a thing as girl push-ups

in the army. There weren't. Of course she could do regular push-ups—she never referred to them as man push-ups—but she didn't want to put down her plate of pretty appetizers to prove it at a party.

She was relieved to have remained Ballerina Baby tonight. She bid Drummer a fond adieu.

His response was different than his usual "looking forward to it." Now that I know you are alive and safe, I'll be able to sleep tonight. Lock your doors and don't talk to strangers, ok?

She hadn't done such a good job making him feel better, after all.

Drummer wasn't worried that she'd get caught in a hurricane or a tornado, nor something as common and simple as a car accident. He was worried that she'd be a victim of an assault and battery. She was the least likely woman to be a victim of a crime—not impossible, but not probable.

You, too, she wrote. By the way…

Yes?

This concern for my safety has me thinking about women in general, and crime statistics in general. Are you worried about me just because I'm a woman?

She watched the cursor blink once. Twice. Three times.

No. I'm worried about you because you're important to me, Baby. If anything bad happened to you, it would be bad for me, too.

Chloe felt her heart beating, hard, in time with the blinking of the cursor.

After long seconds, she typed one word: Same.

Lame. She was so lame. She carried her laptop into her

bedroom, closed it and plugged it in to its docking station. The sound of its familiar click brought tears to her eyes.

Tears? She refused to cry as she pulled a nightgown out from the drawer below her PT uniforms. It was just a click. Nothing but a stupid click.

It was all she had.

Drummer was the perfect guy. He genuinely cared about her. She had a friend in him, a confidant, but every time she went to bed, she was alone.

She crawled into bed and lay silently in the dark, when what she wanted to do was rage at the universe that life was unfair. She couldn't take a laptop to dinner and a movie. She couldn't kiss a laptop. She was twenty-two years old. She wanted more. She wanted passion. She wanted *sex*, but it had to be with someone who meant something to her.

Not possible. The only man she was interested in was the one in her laptop.

She tried to imagine what it would be like if her virtual boyfriend became reality. She'd have a man to rest against. Maybe they'd fall asleep together while spooning, her back to his chest.

Chloe felt herself drifting off to sleep, lulled by her own fantasy. He'd have his arm around her waist, and she'd know when he was falling asleep because the weight of his arm would grow heavier.

She snuggled the side of her face into her pillow, almost smiling as she imagined snuggling with her nameless, faceless *him*. She would be warm when she spooned against him, maybe too warm, but she wouldn't move because she loved falling asleep like this, knowing that the last face she saw before she fell asleep would be the first face she'd see when she woke up.

He'd have a handsome face. Very handsome, with light-colored eyes that crinkled at the corners a bit because he was smiling at her, enjoying every word she said, laughing at every joke.

Chloe jerked awake.

That was Thane Carter's face. Wrong man. So very wrong, and she needed him to get out of her head. She punched her pillow once, twice, and tried to fall back asleep.

Damn it.

She wished that she'd never laid eyes on First Lieutenant Thane Carter. He already made her real life harder. Now he was ruining her imaginary one, too.

Chapter Eleven

Chloe sat at her desk and struggled not to fall asleep in front of Carter.

She'd only been here two weeks, but she'd fallen asleep in her office chair twice. Carter just loved to wake her up. The first time, he'd put his phone on her desk quietly, like a sneaky weasel, then set it off to play the reveille bugle call. The next time, he'd sailed a paper airplane right into her head while he stood in the hallway. Judging from the paper airplanes littering the floor around her desk, it had taken him at least four tries to land a plane on her head—or else he'd hit her four times but she'd been sleeping too hard to notice.

If the paperwork part of her job wasn't so boring, it wouldn't be so hard to stay awake. It would also help if she wasn't trying to stay awake for thirty-six hours at a stretch. She was part of the regular duty officer rotation now. She'd come to one conclusion: there had to be a better way.

A leader didn't bring a problem to his or her superior's attention without also presenting a possible solution. She knew what the sleep-deprivation problem was. She needed to come up with a solution.

"Yo, Carter. Where can I find the schedule for the duty officers?"

"Don't worry, you're done for the month. No more garrison duty. We'll go into training for our combat missions now. This is your last thirty-six hours for two months."

"I wasn't worried. I want to see the old schedule. Is it all laid out on a calendar somewhere?"

It was like pulling teeth to get him to do it, but Carter finally sent a file from his army laptop to hers with the dates and names going back a month. She read it over, mulled it over. When there'd been only three lieutenants, it must have been brutal. With four lieutenants, it was still exhausting.

They weren't at war. They weren't deployed in a volatile part of the world. They weren't even training to handle sleep deprivation in a future war zone. This was just actual sleep deprivation, and she couldn't see a reason to punish themselves physically like this. Instead, there was a very good reason for them not to: they were performing a real law enforcement mission, not rehearsing for one, and that mission required them to make decisions with clear heads, not exhausted ones.

"What are you frowning at?" Carter asked. The man sure did watch her a lot, considering she was only worth talking to if no other single women were around.

Ha—there were no other single women around. She was it. Tough luck for him; she didn't feel like talking. "Nothing."

When Chloe wanted to see a problem, it worked better when she could sketch it out with old-fashioned pencil and paper. Chloe pushed her laptop out of her way and flipped the least-important-looking document on her desk over. The back was a plain white page, beckoning her to find a pencil and make it come alive. She made columns and rows, sketching out a calendar, then wrote in the days of the week. With one eye on the computer screen, she started transferring names and dates, turning them from a list of words on the screen into something she could see as a picture, shading in work with diagonal lines, shading in time off with crosshatches.

"What are you doing?" Carter asked, sounding irritated.

"I'm concentrating."

Out of the corner of her eye, she could see him looking up at the ceiling as if he was praying for patience, but she ignored that and the too-familiar pang in her heart. *Handsome man; hates me.*

It had only been a couple of weeks. She'd get used to it.

A half hour later, she had a new plan. It ought to work, it could work, but she didn't know how to go about presenting it to the level at which it needed to be approved. She looked over at Thane. It would be nice to ask his advice, but he'd made his feelings toward her clear the first night they'd worked together. It was up to her to keep up with him, not for him to mentor her.

Maybe Salvatore would look it over for her. She took her paper and pencil and started out the door.

"Done for the day?" Carter asked.

"Are you done for the day?" she countered. "Then I'm not, either."

Like it or not, she was tied to Thane Carter. They worked together and they had to suffer together, but if her new plan could be implemented, at least they would both get more sleep. Maybe they wouldn't get on each other's nerves so badly if they were well rested.

It was worth a try.

Thane took his place at the conference room table in the battalion headquarters building.

The commanders of each of the companies that made up the battalion were here, as well as the command sergeant-major and the primary members of the battalion staff. Notebooks, pencils, inside jokes and barbs were all brought to the table as everyone waited for the battalion commander, Colonel Stephens, to arrive.

Thane wasn't normally a part of battalion-level meetings. He'd just returned to Fort Hood yesterday after a week with his parents for Thanksgiving. As soon as he'd signed back in, the CO had signed out, taking off for his own week's leave. As the most senior platoon leader in the 584th, Thane also served as the executive officer, or XO.

The XO took over the CO's duties in his absence, so Thane was sitting in his CO's place at the battalion commander's weekly meeting.

It wasn't his first. He enjoyed them. The senior members worked well together, and that attitude transferred all the way down to the newest private.

The operations officer, Major Nord, came in and dropped a notebook onto the table. Right behind him was...Chloe.

The pang in Thane's chest was instant and too familiar. *Pretty woman; hates me.*

Thane ignored that. He'd had no idea Michaels was coming to the meeting today. It made a commander look bad when he didn't know what his own people were up to.

She took a seat behind the major, in a chair against the wall rather than at the table. Why was a butter bar who'd only been in the battalion for three weeks here at a battalion staff meeting? Michaels should have briefed him on her purpose here. Hell, she ought to have given him a heads-up that she'd be here at all. Thane glared at her. She pretended she didn't see him.

"Staff. Atten—*tion.*" The major called the room to attention, and everyone stood, heels together, arms straight by their sides, as the colonel entered the conference room.

"At ease," Colonel Stephens said. He sat at the head of the table, then everyone took their seats. Colonel Stephens looked up one side of the table and down the other, no doubt doing a quick mental roll call of his own staff. He nodded Thane's way. "I see we've got Lieutenant Carter here today."

"Good morning, sir."

"All right, let's get out of here on time for once. S-1. Go."

The S-1 was the staff officer who handled administration for the battalion. As the captain went over his current challenges, Thane found his attention wandering...to Michaels. Why the ever-loving hell was she here? She wasn't taking notes, or else he'd assume she was a Goody Two-shoes who'd asked to sit in for her own professional development.

The S-2 began her report, covering intel and physical security of the property. Finally, thirty minutes into the meeting, the S-3 began his report. Major Nord sat forward in his chair. "As we discussed, sir, we're considering changing the current schedule for the MPDOs."

Thane glanced at Michaels. MPDO, the Military Police

Duty Officer, concerned them personally. Since they were lieutenants, they were the only two in the room who actually pulled that duty.

Major Nord turned and motioned to Michaels to come to the table. She stood to his left. "I've asked Lieutenant Michaels to be present to answer questions. She designed the new schedule."

Holy hell. She'd been here three weeks. *Three weeks.*

Michaels's plan was simple. The lieutenants of two companies would share MPDO duties, making at least eight lieutenants available. They'd be on call for two months instead of one, but they'd serve every eighth day instead of every fourth. This would be less disruptive to each company's training, and it would be less taxing on the individual lieutenants physically. It also meant that lieutenants from one company would be the officer in charge while another company had its usual month of garrison duty, but Michaels pointed out that lieutenants covered shifts for lieutenants from other companies on occasion already.

It took Michaels just minutes to present the idea. She stated her objective, outlined the current course of action and compared it to her alternate course of action, presenting her logic in the same order as a damned battalion-level MDMP, a formal and lengthy process to develop missions.

Total overkill.

Granted, she kept it brief and there was nothing wrong with following that MDMP sequence, but it was overkill for a platoon leader to use the format. It was overkill for a new lieutenant to be here at all.

Then again, this was the girl who'd held court at the grill, decreeing what ketchup and mustard represented while everyone listened. Why shouldn't she stand here and tell a roomful of company commanders that she could schedule their lieutenants more effectively?

The S-3 had already endorsed the plan, obviously, or he wouldn't have had Michaels present it. Thane had to admit that pulling those thirty-six hours less than once a week sounded a hell of a lot better than the way they'd been doing it. Honestly, he didn't know whether to love her or hate her.

Love was out of the question. Hate crept in.

It crept in, and it found a resentful place to stay when the battalion commander turned to Thane and put him on the spot. "You've been pulling these thirty-six-hour days for how long now? How long have you been in my battalion?"

"Two years, sir."

"For two years, you've been pulling these shifts?"

Everyone was looking at Thane as if these shifts were something unusual—or as if he shouldn't have been pulling them for two years.

Thane leaned forward. "That is the job, sir. I execute the mission as assigned. All the lieutenants in the battalion do, one month out of every three."

His battalion CO studied him for a moment. "That's good."

You're damned right, that's good. I didn't whine and complain about it like Michaels.

Colonel Stephens turned back to Major Nord. "I want the thirty-six hours cut down. After they work an overnight, I want the lieutenants to check in with their companies and handle any meetings or paperwork or whatever the hell the commanders want to do with them, but let's get them off duty by 1100 hours. I don't want a bunch of zombies behind the wheel after the flag goes down."

"Yes, sir." Major Nord jotted down the battalion commander's new orders. "Are we adopting the new schedule, as well?"

Colonel Stephens settled back in his chair. "What do you say, Carter? You're the one who's been pulling these thirty-six-hour shifts."

He didn't even glance Michaels's way. "I think it will work, sir."

"Sure it will. It's so simple it makes you wonder why nobody thought of it sooner."

Thane kept his expression neutral. Inside, he was seething at the subtle criticism that Thane hadn't brought this to his attention sooner.

"One company has to suck it down to get started. I know you just finished pulling rotation every fourth day, but are you LTs in the 584th volunteering to keep working another month with the 401st?"

Clearly the battalion commander thought Thane had seen the plan before this meeting. Maybe Thane's CO had. If so, he'd failed to let Thane know whether or not he wanted his lieutenants to commit to another month of shifts. Even if those shifts would be only every eighth day, it would still take each of his lieutenants out of training and keep them on the duty schedule through December. If anyone had planned to take leave over Christmas, they might be forced to change their plans.

Make a decision, Lieutenant. It was a stock phrase, one meant to remind new officers that it was better to make a decision, even if it turned out to be the wrong one, than it was to waffle and never decide. Thane decided. "It looks like a good plan in the long run, sir. We'll suck it down for the next month to put it in motion."

The meeting moved on. Thane listened and contributed appropriately, but his thoughts were still focused on Michaels. On one hand, he admired her ability to see a problem, come up with a solution and present it to the battalion commander. That took chutzpah. That took confidence. And for just one second, as Thane looked at her profile, he remembered walking toward her on that pool deck, drawn like a magnet to that confidence.

He hadn't realized he was staring at her, but she must have felt the weight of his stare, because she glanced at him.

He looked away. She'd gone around him to the S-3. Thane was right there in her office with her. As the senior platoon leader, he was the person she could have come to for input. As her acting XO, he was the person she should have come to before the commander. Hell, just as the guy whose desk was next to hers, he was the man to whom she should have casually mentioned her idea. Why hadn't she?

No reason, except she wanted to catch him off guard. Publicly.

Love her or hate her? She'd tried to make him look bad in front of the battalion commander.

Hate it is, then.

"Michaels!"

Chloe had had enough of that drill sergeant tone to last her for the rest of her life. She turned around to find the person who'd just addressed her as if she were the lowliest plebe. It had better be someone who outranked her, or she'd be pissed.

It was Carter. She was pissed.

He walked up to her. "I hope you're happy."

Big life. Happiness. Drummer respected those goals.

"I hope so, too. Why do you think I'm happy?"

"You succeeded in getting your revenge."

"I succeeded in getting us a more sane duty schedule."

"Never take your XO by surprise like that. You could have at least given me a warning order."

Warning orders were basic communications that alerted units to stand by for new orders. She didn't owe him any warning order. "What would I be getting revenge for?"

"For the flashlight episode. For the way you think I threw you on the radio that first night. Who knows what your beef is? You tell me."

As if she'd open a discussion on how he treated single women with ugly faces when there was nobody better to talk to. That colored her opinion of him, but that was personal. She hadn't let that motivate her to do anything positive or negative, professionally.

Chloe started walking. Carter did, too.

"So, you think I actually developed and presented a new duty officer schedule to the battalion commander *not* to solve a problem but just to get revenge on you for something about radios and flashlights? Let me put your mind at ease, Carter. I could give a rat's tail about those things."

"You should have told me you were attending the staff meeting today. Instead, you went behind my back to the battalion S-3. When does the most junior platoon leader in the whole battalion go hang out with the S-3?" Thane stopped short.

She stopped.

Darn it, she shouldn't have stopped. "What now?"

"You know him from West Point, don't you? The S-3 is a West Pointer."

"He's a major. He had to have graduated, like, when I was in fifth grade. I don't know him. You seriously are paranoid." She held up her right hand and flashed her class ring at him. "This really doesn't communicate directly with the Pentagon. I told you that ring-knocker thing was a myth."

She'd told him that during that long, cozy talk, the day she'd spent with a handsome man who, it turned out, hated her. In silence, she started walking again.

Carter was silent, too, keeping pace beside her.

Controlled confrontation. They had to work together. They had to rely on each other professionally, but right now, they were both seething in silence. This time, she was the one who stopped walking.

He stopped walking.

"I didn't go to the S-3. I went to Salvatore. He liked the plan. We went to the CO together. The CO picked up the phone and called the S-3, and that's when I met Major Nord." It was all on the up-and-up. There'd been no subterfuge involved.

"Why would you go to Salvatore when I'm sitting at the desk next to yours?"

"Because, Carter, you've made your position toward me

perfectly clear from the first ride-along. You say you're not here to be my mentor? Fine. The kindest thing I could say is that you at least set an example, but the truth is, your contempt came through loud and clear when you told me to try to keep up."

"You said all work and no play."

"I am working. You're just mad that I'm keeping up."

She turned on her heel and walked away.

Chapter Twelve

I wanted to talk to you today. Chloe hit Send.

Great. I'm here. Let's talk.

Something happened at work, like six hours ago, and I wished I could talk to you then and there.

You have a phone, Ballerina. I have a phone.

Chloe stared at those words in horror. He wanted to talk? Actually speak? With voices instead of fonts?

She couldn't do that. She just couldn't bare her soul on a telephone. When she saw her words written out in pink, she often had second thoughts before sending them. If they'd been live on the phone the other night, she probably would have blurted out that he didn't need to worry about her because she had an entire police department behind her, and that would have been the end of their relationship as they knew it. Ballerina Baby would never have been the same to Different Drummer.

I can't call you. Talking is not the same as writing. It would change everything. I need to keep you in my life just as we are. I rely on it. She typed fast and hit Send without pausing, rushing the words as if she were blurting them out loud. Pleading out loud.

Seconds ticked by without any blue words.

This was why, this was exactly why, she didn't want to speak to him on the phone. Without having a chance to think through each sentence, she would say the wrong thing.

But blue words appeared. I meant that I write to you from my phone app, and you could do the same. I know you use your laptop, but that's not as handy for you, obviously. If you downloaded the app on your phone, then you could write to me anytime—like six hours ago, when you needed me. If you wrote to me and I was anywhere I could possibly answer you immediately, I would. I don't want things to change, either. I rely on our conversations, too, and this would make it easier to have those conversations.

Chloe lifted her eyes from the laptop screen to the sunset. It was getting cooler now, past Thanksgiving and heading into December. Once the sun went down, she'd have to leave the plastic chair and table she'd bought for her concrete porch and go inside her apartment. The season was changing, and her evening routine had to change with it. Would it be so awful to change how she communicated with Drummer, too?

If she started using her phone, he would be writing to her throughout her day. She tried to imagine sitting at her desk and getting a quick note from him. It would be…warm. Something to offset the presence of—

Carter.

Chloe froze in her chair as she squinted across the parking lot. She'd been looking between two buildings to see the colorful sunset, but some movement on a balcony had drawn her eye to the building on the left. A man with dark hair in a military cut, with shoulders that looked buff even from here, had walked onto his balcony, head bowed, phone in his hand. Good God, that couldn't be Carter, could it?

It could be any military guy. She knew Carter lived in this complex, but she hadn't seen him around. She'd never gone back to the pool, and she'd never tried to find out which of the other five buildings was his.

She held very still, so she wouldn't draw attention to herself as she checked the man out. Whom was she kidding? That was Carter. She'd spent enough hours with him to recognize him anywhere.

He lived on the third floor of his building, just as she lived on the third floor of hers, directly across the parking lot. He stopped staring at his phone, letting his hand drop as if he didn't like what he saw on the screen, and then he looked up—or rather, straight across the parking lot. Toward her.

Goddamn it, goddamn it...

Chloe got up from her chair, carrying the laptop but leaving the wineglass, and ducked into her apartment, sliding the door shut. She pulled the string to close the vertical blinds. Maybe he couldn't tell it was her from a distance. After all, she had the advantage of being able to change her hair from a ballerina bun to loose, long hair. Maybe that was adequate camouflage.

Her heart was pounding. She sank onto her couch and set the laptop in her lap. Her phone was where she'd left it earlier, on her footlocker-turned-coffee-table. She stared at the phone a moment. It was an instrument that could change the best thing in her life to something different. Something better. Something worse.

Her routine was going to change, anyway. Her nightly glass of wine on the porch with Drummer had just gotten blown up. It would never be relaxing again, not when she'd have to keep an eye out for Carter. Why not download the app on her phone? It would be like having an ally in the office, someone with whom she could exchange sardonic observations whenever Carter was being especially Carter-like.

Okay, I'm going to download the app to my phone now.

Chloe hit Send.

Chloe.

That had to be Chloe on that balcony, with that long hair swishing over her shoulders as she disappeared into her apartment.

It's not Chloe, it's Michaels. But he'd forgotten how long her hair was when it was down. The door slid shut behind her, and the sunset's golden beams hit her apartment and reflected off the glass. Michaels had made another rookie mistake by choosing that apartment. In the summer, that direct sunlight was going to overpower her air-conditioning.

He looked down at the phone clenched in his hand. I'm going to download the app.

He tore his mind away from Chloe, happy to be distracted from the sight of long hair swishing in the sunset. This was great news; if Ballerina disappeared again, at least every message he sent would go to both her laptop and her phone, doubling his chances of reaching her.

More pink words demanded his attention. Have you ever gotten your dream job and then found out it's not so dreamy?

He glanced across the parking lot at the closed glass door with the annoyingly bright reflection. Isn't that pretty much every job in the world?

Uh-oh. I didn't realize you didn't like your job, either. Do you ever just want to go crazy and yell "Take this job and shove it"?

(Johnny Paycheck, at every karaoke night in every bar, everywhere. Too easy.) It's not the job. It's the coworkers. Coworker, singular. One lousy coworker is trying to sabotage me.

Are you okay? Is he succeeding?

Her questions brought Thane up short. Since the night he'd worked that domestic and then hadn't been able to reach Ballerina, she'd been repeatedly asking him if *he* was okay. He didn't like Ballerina assuming he was vulnerable. It didn't sit right.

Maybe she imagined him as some weakling. He wished he could tell her he was a soldier—for her own peace of mind, of course. Not for his own pride.

Of course I'm okay. Of course I am.

He was. Although he'd been angry with Chl—Michaels at the staff meeting, Thane was coming out of the whole episode with a much better work schedule.

This coworker won't succeed in making me look bad. It's just a pain in the neck to deal with. Thane refrained from using *she* or *her* to refer to the coworker. Ballerina didn't need to think that he was vulnerable to attacks from a girl. It had nothing to do with his pride.

Okay, it had everything to do with his pride.

Ballerina didn't seem to notice. I hope it's nothing more than a pain in the neck, I really do. This app is taking forever to load onto my phone, by the way. It says the most recent version is from 2014. I bet it's no longer being actively updated. I hate when developers just quit maintaining their apps. I had a yoga app I really loved, and one day, it just wasn't there. The phone had done one of those automatic upgrades overnight, and the old app hadn't been updated to handle it. Poof! It was gone.

Ballerina did yoga, did she? Thane smiled at the clue. He spared one second to glance down at the pool and only half a second to remember how he'd once wondered if Michaels was into yoga. Boy, he'd gotten that wrong. She probably kickboxed opponents for fun.

But Ballerina? She really did do yoga. It fit with what he knew of her. She always found something funny in their mundane conversations, because she wanted to make him laugh. And she wanted to make him laugh because she cared about him. She was the kind of nurturing person who wouldn't want to do anyone any harm. After a day in a patrol car dealing with angry and upset people, he appreciated that. He needed that. He needed Ballerina in his life.

If he told her so, it might sound a bit intense, coming out of the blue when the subject was entirely different. He kept it light. A yoga app? There are a million of them. You must have found another one to replace it.

Well, yes, but it was never the same. I liked things the way they were. It would REALLY never be the same if we had to download a new conversation app. What if we didn't have a chance to switch to a new app before this one went poof? I'd know you were out there somewhere, but I wouldn't be able to find you. I'd have to post one of those personal ads. You know the kind, the ones aimed at perfect strangers that say, "We talked in line at the coffee shop and I fell in love with your shark-tooth necklace." I bet those ads never work.

Thane turned his back on the reflected sunset and leaned against his balcony railing as he typed. The sun was sinking fast. It was turning colder. That one wouldn't work with me. I've never worn a shark-tooth necklace. I'm not sure where to buy a thing like that. Who makes them? Maybe the guy who answers the ad could tell you, and you could tell me.

What kind of necklace do you wear, then?

Dog tags.

The desire to tell her the truth hit him with almost brutal force. He wore dog tags. He was in the service, and he wanted to change the rules of their game. He wanted real names, real jobs, real contact. Ballerina was terrific, but lately, instead of filling the loneliness, talking to her only amplified it.

He knew what had changed. He'd met Chloe Michaels, and now he couldn't stop wanting everything that was missing in his long-distance friendship with Ballerina. A words-only relationship meant there was no smile, no sun-kissed skin, no swish of hair, no sharing of a silly hot dog test.

No sex.

Long-distance relationships were a big part of the military. Couples did stay together through deployments by texting and writing letters just as he and Ballerina did, but there was one important difference. Those couples knew their letter-writing months were temporary. Even if a whole year apart stretched before them, they still knew that they would be reunited.

Thane needed that. Ballerina was like a girlfriend, but she wasn't. He needed to know that someday, he would go on leave and fly across the country just to meet her. He wanted to walk off a plane and be greeted with a hug and a smile. He wanted to know their relationship would continue to grow, because it was the best thing he'd found, and he didn't want it to die a stagnant death.

I don't wear jewelry. Our ad would need to say something like, "My words were in blue and yours were in pink. We talked about everything and I could tell you anything, except my name. That was a mistake, because now I've lost you. If you don't respond to this ad, I'll be wondering where you are for the rest of my life."

A chill settled around him as he looked at the words he'd just sent. This app could stop working without warning. If he lost her, he probably would be crazy enough to try a personal ad, because he'd have nowhere else to even begin a search. Ballerina was right; those ads never worked. Where could he even place an ad aimed at the entire United States? If the app crashed, Ballerina might as well be wiped off the face of the earth.

Thane typed quickly against that cold future. My ad was a little too real, wasn't it? But it will happen. Sooner or later, this app will be obsolete. If we're not going to exchange names and numbers, we should at least give each other an email address. We can keep using this app exclusively, if that's what you want, but we should have a backup just in case. It would leave too big a hole in my life if a computer glitch stole you from me. Can we bend our rules this once? An email address so that we aren't vulnerable?

Thane hesitated before hitting Send. He didn't want her to keep thinking of him as vulnerable. He hit the backspace arrow with his thumb, back, back, back.

An email address so that we won't have our routine upset by a computer glitch one day?

He hesitated again. A routine. He couldn't call a girl a routine. That was no way to woo a woman. Back, back, back, before he could fall back into his fantasy of having an actual woman to woo. Woo? Sheesh.

An email address so that a programmer's laziness doesn't tear us apart without warning?

He hit Send.

The cursor blinked in silence.

He hadn't been persuasive enough; she was taking too long to think about it. She didn't want anything to change. She'd been crystal clear about that, but exchanging email addresses really wouldn't have any effect at all. It was just extra insurance that they'd be able to remain online friends. He wanted more, true, but he also couldn't lose what they had.

Thane gave in to the evening chill and went back inside his apartment to try again. Don't be afraid that I'll start spamming your inbox. It's only to have in case the app crashes. Trust me, an email address won't change a thing.

Pink letters spelled out an email address, highlander@ ctx.com.

Thane tapped the email address quickly, as if it were going to disappear, and created a new contact for it in his phone. First name: Ballerina. Last name: Baby.

There, she was safe in his phone. Adding her to the list of people he interacted with every day made her more real than ever. She was a contact he could reach with an email address that ended *@ctx.com*, the same as half the soldiers in his platoon.

Half his soldiers?

They had that same ending on their email addresses because *ctx* stood for Central Texas. The suffix *@ctx.com* was a popular internet provider's domain name, a company out of Austin.

Ballerina lived near him.

Thane slowly sat on his couch, keeping his eyes on his phone, not daring to adjust his grip on the device. It was like a grenade that was about to go off.

This changed everything. Thank God.

He hesitated, thumbs over the screen. She was afraid of change; he needed to break this to her gently.

Hey, BB, you know how we've wondered whether this app matched us up by design or by pure luck?

Yes?

I think it was by design.

Why?

Because I recognize the @ctx.com part of your email address. We both live in the Austin area.

Nothing, just a white screen.

He typed in his email address for her. It ended with @gmail.com. That domain name could be from anywhere in the world. If she'd had one of those email addresses, too, a gmail or even an old aol.com, they'd never know they lived in the same state.

But she'd used ctx.com, so she was either in Austin or somewhere reasonably close, like Temple or Waco.

Or here in Killeen.

Thane stood to pace. She was his closest friend, his favorite person to talk to, and now…she could be more. This was incredible. This was fantastic.

This is awful, she wrote.

Thane stopped pacing. It's a lot of things, but not awful.

She didn't reply. He ran one hand up the back of his neck as he waited.

Hey, Ballerina? You there? Don't go silent on me. Please. As soon as he hit Send, he regretted it. That had sounded too much like begging, like a vulnerable man begging. He needed to keep it light. If you disappear now, I'll have to take those personal ads out all over Austin.

Silence.

He tried again. The only quotes I can think of about silence are from Simon & Garfunkel. Please don't make me write out the lyrics to "Sound of Silence." Short version: silence sucks.

At last, she responded. I can't catch my breath. Don't you see? This feels like the app crashed, after all. Ballerina and Drummer as we knew it just changed. Forever.

Chapter Thirteen

Chloe chucked the live hand grenade as far as she could, then dived behind the dirt berm with the NCO in charge of this position on the firing line. The explosion vibrated the earth. Dirt sprinkled from the sky onto her Kevlar helmet.

For the first time in forty-eight hours, she smiled. Sometimes, when everything was going wrong, a girl just needed to blow crap up.

"Nice throw, ma'am."

"Thanks, Sergeant."

"Most women don't throw that well."

And…poof. There went her good mood. "Seriously, Sergeant? Should I give you the formal lecture on gender bias, or should I just point out that the only person who's failed to qualify so far today was a guy?"

The soldier to their right threw his grenade. Chloe and the sergeant stayed crouched behind their berm with their heads down, but they knew the grenade hadn't gone very far and hadn't gone very straight, because the explosion shook the earth hard and dirt rained down on them.

They cussed in unison.

"Make that two men who failed," the sergeant muttered.

Chloe almost laughed. "I'm going to be very fair and not say that most men don't throw well, even though those two suck."

The sergeant chuckled, maybe a little nervously, maybe a little relieved. "You've got a point there, ma'am."

The order to clear the firing line came from the loudspeakers on the tower.

Chloe stood up and dusted herself off. "All right. I'm outta here. Stay safe—especially when those two come back on the line to try again."

Chloe cleared the range and returned to the little set of

wood bleachers behind the firing line. As she took out her ear plugs, other members of the 584th took their places by the berms, waited for their commands from the tower—which was more like a lifeguard stand—and then threw their hand grenades, one at a time. Everyone on the bleachers booed and cheered the throws, acting more like fans at a baseball game than soldiers practicing the use of a deadly close-quarters-combat weapon.

Chloe's grenade-induced adrenaline buzz faded as she drank from her canteen. Explosions were all well and good, but it didn't change the fact that her relationship with Drummer had come to an abrupt end.

Drummer didn't get it. No, Ballerina. This is the opposite of a crash. Instead of disappearing, now we can actually appear. In person.

Night after night, she'd been going to bed lonely, angry that the only man she cared about was stuck in her laptop. Now, she was angry that he was so eager to jump out of that laptop and kill this friendship.

Don't you want to meet, Baby?

No.

His silence after that had been awful, which was why, exactly why, she was afraid to talk to him live. She could be too direct, something that was good in the military, but bad in every other aspect of life. She'd hurt Drummer with that curt *no*.

The only way to explain herself was to lay her insecure soul bare. What if we met and you decided you didn't like me?

Not possible.

That was very sweet, but very wrong. It was quite possible

that he wouldn't like her. It happened to her all the time, in situations where she least expected it. She'd just had a nice surprise insult from the sergeant on the firing line. The last time she'd gone to church with her parents, she'd worn her dress blue uniform, and a lovely little old lady had hissed at her that she was stealing a job from a man.

Drummer wouldn't be mad at her for being a girl...but he might not like the fact that she was a soldier.

He might not like that she was in law enforcement, either. Just this week, Chloe had stopped her patrol car behind a motorist with a flat tire. The driver had started ranting and raving at her before she'd even walked up to him, furious that she'd stopped to ticket him for blocking traffic. It hadn't even occurred to her to give him a ticket. She'd stopped because her red and blue flashing lights would keep him safer from oncoming traffic while he changed his tire.

Three more grenades were thrown. Each explosion vibrated the cold plank she sat on. The next three soldiers filed onto the firing line. Even in his helmet and combat gear, Carter was easy to recognize. Something about his height or the set of his shoulders...

Thane Carter. There was another person she'd thought liked her, but he'd decided she sucked. He was even pissed off that she'd developed a better work schedule for him.

It's always possible for someone not to like me, she'd written to Drummer last night.

His answer had been direct. Tell me what about you is unlikable. In six months of near-daily conversations, I haven't seen it yet.

She'd paused, hands poised over her laptop keys. He might not like her because she was...what? She wasn't a bad person. She wasn't a bad cop. She didn't even look bad in a mirror. She'd had another moment of clarity on her bright red couch: she liked herself.

She just could never predict when someone else wouldn't.

The range ended too soon. The NCO in charge hustled

the troops through a trash detail, then called them into formation and marched them out to the dirt parking lot. Chloe didn't need to look toward Carter for a clue about what to do. She already knew when a sergeant ordered troops to fall in line, he wasn't addressing commissioned officers. She walked behind the formation with Carter.

They didn't speak. They had nothing to talk about.

The parking lot was empty. The troops were here. The trucks were not. *Hurry up and wait* was the army way. Everyone sat on the ground in place to wait, helmets off, phones in more hands than not. Chloe didn't feel like sitting. It was nice, as an officer, to have the prerogative to stay on her feet and pace a little bit behind the troops.

Carter was doing the same. The frosty silence between them continued, until Carter pulled out his personal cell phone. Chloe pulled out hers. If Carter could do it, she could do it.

She checked her app. Drummer still thought meeting in person was a great idea—and his flashing icon indicated he was online right now.

She typed as quickly as she could on her phone. What if we meet and have nothing to talk about?

That won't happen. It can't. Star Trek can be endlessly dissected, if nothing else.

A laugh escaped her. The soldiers didn't seem to notice, but Carter looked at her sharply.

Jeez. She was allowed to laugh in uniform. She turned her back to Carter, and gave her attention to the man who didn't disapprove of her. Yet.

Thane was as hungry and tired as every other soldier by the time the trucks finally pulled into the parking lot.

Hungry, tired…and hopeful. Ballerina seemed to be adjusting to the idea that they lived too close not to meet. Not even a long, uncomfortable ride in the back of a troop transport could dampen his spirits now.

Ballerina was in the middle of doing something. She kept dropping quick BRBs, the acronym for *Be Right Back*. Thane imagined her at a dance rehearsal, stealing moments between scenes to check her phone, the way he was stealing moments to check his.

He pocketed his phone to vault into the back of the truck and take a place on a hard bench. He looked around at the soldiers and tried to imagine a dance troupe instead. A ballerina...her hair must be up in a bun, exposing a graceful neck. She'd be intent upon her work, physically strenuous work, so perhaps she'd have a fine sheen of sweat on a clean face. Really, not so different from a female soldier.

With a jolt, he realized his gaze had drifted to Chloe Michaels. She really was quite pretty and her hair was always tightly pulled back like a ballerina, and—

Michaels plopped her Kevlar helmet on her head and fastened the chin strap.

So much for that.

The truck took off. Thane checked his phone.

The ctx email address I gave you is new. It's not the one I had when I first signed up for this app. We weren't matched up because we both live in Austin.

But you live near Austin now? Thane asked.

Yes, but I'm not what you think I am.

Not human? Not female? Not in your 20s?

I'm all those things, but I'm not a native Texan.

I'm not, either.

I'm not a ballerina.

I'm not, either.

At the opposite end of the truck bed, he heard Michaels snort in amusement at something on her phone screen.

Thane returned to his phone, but he felt impatient. He was done with phone screens. He glanced at Michaels again, at her graceful neck and her elegant profile. He wanted a real woman, a real dinner, a real conversation, and he knew exactly whom he wanted to have it with.

Ballerina Baby.

Baby, doesn't it drive you crazy that the app knows something about us that we don't know? Let's get together and figure out why this app matched us up.

He waited. The brown scenery went by, uninteresting, flat. The diesel engine droned on. Then his phone vibrated in his hand, two shorts and a long.

I guess I'm just delaying the inevitable. How do you want to meet?

How? ASAP.

Thane kicked back on his couch. Thursday night in December meant an NFL game was on, same old routine.

December means the Nutcracker. I'm not a ballerina, but I do love the ballet.

But this Thursday, he was making plans to meet Ballerina, and that was most definitely something new.

He'd told her months ago that he'd never seen a live ballet, so now she suggested they meet in Austin at a ballet performance: I guarantee you'll recognize every single piece of music in the second half. I just hold my breath the whole time, one great dance after another. It's a celebration of the most luxurious foods from around the world.

Wait—the Nutcracker ballet is about food?

Ballerina was the only friend with whom he could learn something new about ballet while watching an NFL game. She had the game on, too, but she wasn't impressed with the lackluster offense. Neither was he. The ballet convo was more absorbing than watching another punt.

Coffee is represented by a sort of Flamenco ballet in Spanish costumes, for example.

Thane chuckled, alone in his apartment. I thought ballets were supposed to be romantic. It's about food? I can get behind coffee.

Well, it's supposed to be a kind of paradise, see? The nutcracker has become a prince, and he wants Clara to have the best of everything. Coffee is one of the best things in life, so it really is romantic.

I love a girl who thinks food is romantic. Is there a dance for steak and potatoes?

No—it's flowers. Sugar plums and mirlitons.

What's a mirliton? Never mind. I'm in.

Together, they logged on to the ticketing website. Together, they decided which seats to get. She insisted on paying for her own. Thane couldn't really stop her from buying Mezzanine D130 for herself, so he bought Mezzanine D131, and silently vowed that he'd be paying for dinner and drinks and anything else she wanted to do the rest of the night. The rest of the weekend.

The rest of their lives.

I'm looking forward to it, Baby.

"Friday night. Almost quitting time, Boss." Sergeant First Class Lloyd walked into Thane's office. "Do you have big plans for the weekend, sir?"

Thane could speak freely, because Michaels had left about fifteen minutes ago. "Yes, Sergeant First Class, as a matter of fact, I do."

"Kicking ass and taking names?"

"Not until next week." Again, since Michaels had left, Thane could speak freely. "That new duty officer schedule is a godsend. I have actual weekends."

"Whiskey and women then, sir?"

"Wom*an*. Singular. Just one."

Lloyd pulled Michaels's desk chair over with a squeak of wheels. "I didn't even know you were dating anyone. Is this exclusive?"

"After tomorrow night, it will be."

Lloyd cleared his throat before adopting a fatherly tone. "This sounds serious, Lieutenant Carter."

"It is."

It felt good, really good, to say he was serious about Ballerina. Thane had never been more serious about a girl in his life.

"My wife is going to want all the details, sir. How long have you known this woman?"

"Since June."

"But—" Lloyd sat back, incredulous. "You never—"

"We've been friends since June, just friends." Thane didn't bring up pen pals. He didn't want to have to defend an online-only relationship. It wouldn't be online-only for much longer, anyway. "But this weekend, we're taking it to the next level. I want to do this right, a big night out. I'm taking her to the *Nutcracker* in Austin, for starters."

Sergeant First Class Lloyd got one of those grins on his face, like he knew something that Thane didn't know. "When a man looks as excited as you do about going to the ballet, the woman must be something special. How special are we talking, sir?"

If she's even one-quarter as funny and smart and caring and happy as I think she is...who can resist happiness?

"If this weekend goes the way I think it will, I could be buying a diamond ring for someone as a Christmas gift."

Chapter Fourteen

Seat D130.

She'd be sitting in D130. Thane's heart pounded as he headed up the stairs to the mezzanine level. He could run this flight of stairs without breaking a sweat, but knowing each stair brought him closer to Ballerina Baby made his heart pound in a way exercise didn't.

He was stuck going at a snail's pace, moving with the crowd of folks dressed for the holidays, little girls with tinsel in their hair, little boys wearing their first neckties. Red and green, silver and gold were the colors of Christmas, but Ballerina had told him she'd wear something pink and blue, like the words that made up their friendship.

Thane scanned the crowd, looking for pink and blue in the holiday-colored sea that flowed steadily upward. He'd dressed for an Austin Saturday night at the theater, navy blazer and a dress shirt, no tie, with dark-washed jeans. Like most of the men, he wore polished cowboy boots, because he'd lived in Texas for years now, and he was taking a girl out on the town tonight.

He reached the top of the stairs. The mezzanine level's lobby was simple, a carpeted space between the theater doors to his right and a glass wall to his left. Beyond the glass, the view of Austin at night was the star of the show.

It couldn't hold his attention. Thane walked straight to the theater doors, waving off the program an usher held out. The house lights were still up. Conversation among those finding their seats provided a background hum of pleasant expectations. Individual instruments were being tuned in the orchestra pit, their random notes adding to that sense of building excitement.

Thane headed down the aisle toward the balcony railing. Row D would be only four rows from the front edge. Ballerina had preferred being in the center of row D rather than off to one side of row A. She'd written passionately about being able to see the entire scene and symmetry of the choreography from the center; she really loved this ballet.

Thane put his hand on the railing, feeling a sense of vertigo as he headed down the aisle at the crowd's pace, keeping an eye on the letters that designated the seating. Row I, row H, row G.

He hadn't felt this lightness or eagerness or whatever it was since…well, since that poolside afternoon with Chloe. He'd been so certain, so sure that person was going to be part of his life, a good part. The ground had dropped out from under him when he'd realized she was his fellow platoon leader. That onslaught of vertigo had been sickening.

This vertigo was intoxicating. This was pure anticipation. This was Ballerina. He'd known her for six months, not one afternoon. He knew her likes and dislikes, her sense of humor, her favorite shows and songs. He knew she cared for him. He knew her heart's desire was to have more friends, her goal in life was happiness.

This was it. The real it. The one woman who might end his bachelor days.

Row D, at last.

Thane started to sidestep his way toward the middle. D117, 118…

He lifted his eyes, his heart in his throat. The seats in the middle were still empty. Beyond them, people were coming down the aisle on the opposite side. A white-haired couple, a young family, a beautiful woman in black, eye-catchingly beautiful—

That woman in black.

Michaels?

It took him a second, but he recognized her. Her black dress reminded him of an ice-skater, with a pastel bow tied around her waist before the skirt flared out. As always, just the sight of her made his jaw clench and his muscles tense.

Her hair was pinned up, but not pulled back as tightly as usual. It was looser, softer, and a few pieces had come down and were sort of wavy. *Tendrils*, that was the word.

Thane stopped as she continued down the far aisle. For the love of—what the *hell* was Michaels doing here? This was worse, exponentially worse, than the way she'd shown up without warning at the battalion staff meeting. Not only was Michaels at the same performance, she was going to sit in the mezzanine, disrupting his night like she disrupted everything else. Now how was she going to attack him, undermine him, make him miserable? He didn't want to deal with Michaels and her damned perfect *tendrils* when he was dying to meet someone else.

"Are you going to pass me or not?" A man in the seat before him had twisted sideways to give him room.

"Sorry."

But Thane took only one more step before stopping, watching in horror as Michaels entered row D from the other side. Good God, what were the odds? This was insane. It was the biggest night of his life, the night when he was finally going to meet the woman of his dreams, and Michaels was here to make it all difficult.

He retreated. He backed out of the row and went back up a few steps, row E, row F, going upstream against the flow of people. He paused there. He'd let Michaels take her seat, then he'd go back in and be careful not to look toward her end of the row as he took his seat in the center. If he didn't make eye contact, he wouldn't have to acknowledge her existence at all.

He watched Michaels pass seat after seat after seat, smiling and nodding thanks as she worked her way into the row, his horror growing as she got closer and closer to the center of the row, right to where he and Ballerina were going to meet.

No.

Michaels was wearing black, not pink and blue. It was a

freak coincidence that she was standing in the center of the row. She'd probably entered from the wrong side and would keep moving to this end, to a seat near his aisle.

The house lights dimmed halfway. Patrons started hustling toward their seats in earnest. Michaels stayed where she was, right in the center, and sat down.

Thane didn't move as the world dropped out from under him.

Then anger propelled him. Thane turned to walk up a few more rows. He didn't want Michaels to see him. He'd wait, out of the way, until he saw Ballerina show up, because Michaels was not, could not be, Ballerina.

He stomped up to row G. Row H.

Not. Possible.

There'd been some mistake. Thane turned around and leaned his back against the wall, leaving room for others to continue past him. He focused fiercely on the row closest to the railing. That was A. The next one back was B, then C, and…D. No mistake. Michaels was sitting in D. In the center.

He glared daggers at the back of her head, hating all those tendrils and curls and *flowers*. His heart contracted hard in his chest; those flowers in her hair were pink and blue.

Ballerina was Michaels.

The house lights went dark. The chair to her left remained empty. The orchestra continued tuning up, the random, discordant notes from individual instruments screeching into his skull.

An usher with a flashlight asked Thane if he needed help finding his seat. Thane grabbed the program from the usher and sat in the closest seat that was open. He watched Michaels look down her row to her left, then to her right.

He refused to feel guilty. Michaels wouldn't exactly jump for joy if he came sidling through row D and took Drummer's seat. She'd have a heart attack. She hated him as much as he hated her.

The conductor raised his baton; the overture began. Thane

wasn't directly behind Michaels, but off to the side, so he could see a little bit of her profile. Her face was illuminated by the light of her cell phone as she typed something rapidly. Her earring sparkled as it reflected the phone's light, then she tucked a curl behind her ear. Her hair was disconcertingly feminine, a few little braids holding the flowers among those loose curls. It looked like something a bride would wear.

Total overkill.

Typical Michaels. He hoped she hadn't paid money to have her hair done like that. Tonight was just supposed to be a meet and greet. She'd placed way too much importance on the whole thing. She'd taken it too seriously.

The curtain rose, and she turned off the too-bright light of her phone screen. The audience applauded. Thane's phone buzzed in the inner pocket of his blazer. Two shorts and a long.

No way in hell was he going to check that. All those months of pink words, all that hope he'd placed on them, and she'd been lying to him the whole time. Her personality in real life was nothing like she'd been online. There was a word for that, for people who developed fake online personalities just to see if they could capture someone's devotion: *catfishing*. She'd catfished him, damn it.

He stewed, he steamed, he looked at her and then resolutely looked at the stage instead. Ten eternally long minutes later, the people onstage were still dancing at a stupid party. Not even dancing—it was just slow walking. There was no point to it, just a parade of historical gowns.

He wished he'd never come.

He wished the app had crashed.

I would have spent my whole life wondering where you are.

He was spared that much, at least. He knew exactly where she was—and he wished like hell he didn't.

Michaels looked to her left one more time. She looked to her right again. *Clear on the right.* She wasn't even watch-

ing the ballet she supposedly loved so much. She was looking for him, her little catfish victim.

She'd have to keep looking. Drummer was a definite no-
show.

The interminably long ballet kept going and going. Onstage, a rat with a crown on its head was tiptoeing around a
bed. Who thought of this stuff? It was as unfathomable as
everything else this night. A lame swordfight followed between the rat and the nutcracker. Thane watched the back
of Michaels's head as she dropped her chin to look down to
her lap. A quick flash of light followed. She'd checked the
phone, of course.

To see if I answered. Me, of all people.

The woman to the right of Michaels shifted angrily in her
seat and held her hand up in an exaggerated way to block
the light. The phone went dark immediately, but Michaels's
profile was lit now by the white light from the stage as fake
snow started to fall.

He could see her face clearly. It was easy to read her lips
as she said, "I'm sorry." She bowed her head. She didn't
even look at the stage.

Neither did Thane. He looked at her and all the sorrow
on her face, the—*hurt.*

Thane scrubbed his hand over his jaw, so recently shaved
for a woman he'd thought he knew. He couldn't look at Michaels's bowed head, at the sad curve of her mouth. Instead,
he stubbornly looked at the stage, where, finally, what he
recognized as ballet was taking place. Dozens of women in
white tutus and white pointe shoes were striking ballet poses
in a snowstorm for some reason, jumping in a formation of
two rows so perfectly aligned, they put the military to shame.
For a second, one flash of a second, Drummer thought how
easy it was going to be to tell Ballerina something he could
genuinely appreciate about her beloved ballet.

One millisecond later, he remembered who Ballerina
was, and he couldn't take the flash of pain, not one more

time. He was on his feet without thinking, sidestepping out of the aisle, ignoring dirty looks from the usher and sneaking out the door.

Chapter Fifteen

Thane's phone buzzed in his pocket, two shorts and a long.

He wasn't going to look at that app ever again.

The mezzanine lobby was mostly empty except for the bartenders at a bar set up at one end. The Austin city lights were bright, a view that would be romantic in other circumstances. Any other circumstance.

He knew he should leave, but he sank onto the only furniture in the place, a long bench covered in black leather. What a frigging disaster this night had turned out to be.

So why wasn't he leaving Michaels in the middle of her little row in the middle of her little ballet?

The theater doors to his left and right opened, and people began pouring out for intermission. Thane opened his program, prepared to duck behind it as he kept an eye out for Michaels. He needed to know where she was in order to avoid her.

There. She walked right past him in pair of high-heeled sandals, deadly-looking stiletto heels.

He didn't look away; he needed to keep track of her. Her skirt ended well above her knee. Between her hemline and her pink-polished toes, her nude legs drew his eye. She moved differently in high heels than she did in combat boots, that was for sure. He'd always thought she was pretty, but he hadn't seen her legs since that day by the pool, when she'd been barefoot in a sports bikini. Tonight, in high heels, she looked…elegant.

All right, she looked sexy. Then again, high heels made a woman's legs, any woman's legs, look sexy. The last thing Thane needed to see was a sexy Chloe Michaels. He resented her for looking so good, all dressed up for a night on the town with a man. With him.

If she'd known it was him, she wouldn't have come here at all.

He was leaving, damn it, but she was leaving first, heading straight for the stairs with quick steps. Her skirt swished around her thighs and she moved as lightly on those high heels as if she wore them all the time, when he knew for a fact she did not. She nearly ran down the stairs, disappearing from his view, her hand barely touching the rail.

He didn't care where she was going. For at least sixty seconds, he sat still, telling himself he didn't care. It would probably be safe for him to leave using the opposite stairs. But his phone felt heavy in his jacket pocket. Had she left him a message—had Ballerina left Drummer a message—telling him where she was going?

Thane stood up to leave.

And pulled his phone out. White screen, pink letters. I know cell reception in this building is spotty, but if you get this, stay in your seat. I just realized there is a D130 at orchestra level. I'm in D130 on the mezzanine level. I'll come down and find you. I'm so sorry for the confusion! I'm here, I promise.

He slid his phone back in his jacket. He had every intention of going down the stairs and out to the parking garage, but instead he went back into the theater. The house lights were up, bright. He stayed close to the wall, cursing his own curiosity with every row he passed, until he stood at the balcony railing.

Down below, to the right, were the doors closest to the stairs Michaels had just taken. Row D had to be close to the stage. Everyone who was going to leave for intermission had left at this point. Perhaps only a quarter of the audience remained in their seats, so it was easy to spot Michaels as she walked in.

The sorrow had been replaced by an expectant look. She smiled, radiant with hope, and Thane felt his heart contract again. This was wrong, all so wrong. She was going to be disappointed in just a minute. Whoever was sitting in Orchestra D131 was not him.

It was like watching an accident unfold in slow motion. She found the right row. She tugged her dress into place, fingertips grazing that pale pink ribbon around her waist as she looked down the mostly empty row. Thane glanced down it, too. There were a few elderly folks still seated. A middle-aged man, too, probably twice her age with the beginnings of a bald spot, easy to see from above. Chloe kept a determined smile on her face and scooted her way down the aisle. She made contact, polite conversation with a sweet smile. She touched the sleeve of the man with the bald spot, and from here, Thane would have sworn he saw the word *Drummer* on her lips.

No?

No, the man shook his head.

She nodded, she gave the group a little wave, and she turned around to walk out. Thane looked, really looked, and he saw Ballerina walking away, light on her feet, hair done up in feminine flowers, skirt swirling around her thighs. Ballerina.

His fantasy. If Drummer had been any other man in Central Texas, he would've been suckered into believing that this graceful Ballerina was authentic. She wasn't, and Thane knew it. He sat beside her in the office, rode beside her in troop transports and coordinated company exercises with her. He knew the sound of her voice over the radio in his HUMM-V and over the radio in his patrol car. He *knew* Michaels. That girl down there was a fake, deceiving a man who'd been nothing but kind and supportive to her since June.

The audience began filing in again. The orchestra started tuning up. Thane sidestepped the entire length of the balcony railing to the far side of the mezzanine, just to avoid the woman he'd come to see—the woman who'd come to see him, with hope and anticipation written all over her face. Her disappointment had been equally obvious.

So is mine.

Thane headed for the lobby, his feet feeling heavier with every step. There was no one to talk to, no one to see. The lobby was almost empty, except for the bar in the corner. Thane headed over.

The bartender nodded toward Thane. "What can I get you, sir?"

With a lift of his chin, Thane indicated the whiskey bottle on display. "Single. On the rocks."

So few words to sum up so much.

Chloe returned to the mezzanine level at a more sedate pace. She wasn't going to let her hopes rise too high, not again, but as she walked down the aisle to row D, she looked toward the center. Maybe, finally...

Her seat was empty. The one next to hers was empty, too.

"Are you coming in or not?" The man in the aisle seat had done the usual half twist to tuck his legs to one side.

Chloe mustered up a polite smile. "No, sorry. I'm not going to...no. Sorry."

She dragged herself back up the stairs, reached the lobby and checked her phone. Again.

She didn't have much of a signal, so she walked closer to the windows and held her phone out. Maybe her messages hadn't been sent yet. Maybe they were all piling up, waiting until she caught a better signal. Maybe Drummer's phone was being just as unreliable. Maybe the performing arts center's Wi-Fi had been overwhelmed by a thousand phones at intermission.

She turned off her phone's Wi-Fi and switched to cellular data, hope rising in her heart just one more time.

She stood there with her hand outstretched, staring at the white screen like it was a crystal ball, until her hand started to tremble.

She was a fool.

Behind her, a pair of long black leather benches ran parallel to the glass wall. She sank down on one and stared out at the city lights as the lobby emptied and the theater filled. At least the view of Austin didn't disappoint her. Everything else, every single other thing, did.

She didn't have the heart to go back in the theater and sit with that empty seat beside her for another hour. The last hour of her life had been miserable as she'd stared at the stage, trapped between the empty seat to her left and an angry woman to her right. Not that she could blame the woman. A bright cell phone screen was inexcusable in a dark theater, but Chloe had checked her phone because she'd felt so desperate. Quietly desperate.

They say most men lead lives of quiet desperation. But you're not like most men.

Yes, she was. She would have given anything for anyone, anyone at all to come fill that empty seat. Someone too old, too young, handsome or plain, too thin, too fat, someone who talked brashly or stuttered shyly—she didn't care. It would have been Drummer, and if she'd felt no romantic spark with him, she still would have had someone to talk to. She still would have connected with a human being who wanted to know her instead of waiting with that awful, achingly empty seat beside her.

"Michaels? Is that you?"

Good God. Thane Carter. She focused on the city view and pretended she hadn't heard him.

He walked right up to her, blocking the view. "It is you. Mind if I sit down?" He didn't wait for her answer, but sat on the bench with her. She scooted away a few inches, but she couldn't go far, because she was on the end of the bench. Jeez, he didn't have to sit right beside her on this one. Right next to her was an entire second bench.

"I'm—I'm waiting on someone, actually." She looked over her shoulder at the last few stragglers who hadn't gone back into the theater. Drummer could still show up. There might have been an accident on I-35, all lanes closed, traffic redirected, detoured through side streets. Drummer, of course, would have too much common sense to try to check his phone or type her a message while he was behind the wheel.

Carter looked over his shoulder, too. "Where is he? I assume it's a he?"

She sat up a little straighter and looked back out the window.

"Big secret?" he pressed. "Hot date? Must be a hot date. I've never seen you so…" He had the nerve to flap his hand in her general direction, from her head to her lap. "So…girly."

"Could you please leave?"

He held up a glass tumbler of ice and amber liquid. "As soon as I've finished my whiskey."

"Shouldn't you be in the theater with whatever woman you came here with?"

"You know, it's possible I came by myself, because I enjoy the ballet."

"No, it isn't."

"No, it isn't." He frowned and took a slow, deliberate taste of his drink.

She stopped watching his lips on the glass and folded her arms across her chest, her usual defensive posture around him. "Is she even here?"

"Oh, she's here, all right." Carter's gaze dropped to her folded arms for the barest of seconds, then back to the Austin view.

Chloe looked down. Crap. Folding her arms in uniform was no big deal. Maybe it even gave her a little tough swagger. But in a dress with a V-neck, it emphasized her cleavage. She dropped her hands to her lap, then the bench. She felt the pink satin ribbon under her fingers and smoothed it out. The ribbon was such a sign of how desperate she was not to miss Drummer. She'd been afraid the flowers in her hair weren't obvious enough, so she'd stopped at the flower stand in the lobby to buy a yard of satin ribbon to tie in a bow around her waist, so that her black dress wouldn't be so black. *Quiet desperation.*

"How about you?" Thane asked. "Don't you want to get back inside and see the rest of the show? I bet you love the second half."

She frowned at his mocking tone.

He kept it up. "I bet you think people interpreting the emotions of candy canes and gingerbread makes perfect sense. I bet you call it art when it's nothing more than holiday tripe."

She gasped at his attack. "Yes, it's art. Art doesn't have to be tragic."

"It does if art imitates life."

"*The Nutcracker Suite* is some of the most thrilling choreography set to some of the most stirring music ever written. It's a lighthearted subject and a joyful setting, but that doesn't negate the fact that it is a work of genius that millions of people have enjoyed for over a century."

Carter raised an eyebrow at her lecture, then raised his highball glass in a toast.

She relaxed the tiniest bit.

"There's no plot." He tossed back a swig, not a sip, of the whiskey. "It's a boring Christmas party followed by a snowstorm and dancing candy."

This was just what she needed, a horrible, emotional evening capped off by Carter insulting one of her favorite things in life. She could have cheerfully shoved his butt off the bench with her stilettoed foot, but instead she slid the last inch away from him and sat on the end of the bench in silence.

She debated whether or not Carter would consider it a victory if she moved to the second bench until the glass window reflected movement at the staircase. She looked toward the stairs and blocked out everything and everyone except the man coming up the steps. He was a little frumpy and rumpled, but harmless-looking. Could he be Drummer?

The man called out to one of the lobby stragglers, then walked over to shake hands with him.

She let out the breath she'd been holding.

"Who are you looking for?" Carter looked around her to the staircase. "Don't you know where your date is?"

"I'm not on a date."

"Really? This is how you dress when you go out by yourself?"

The man hated her. First her face, now her dress. She hardened her heart, or she tried to. It was difficult when her feelings were already so battered. "I'm not on a date, but I'm not by myself. I'm expecting someone, and I'd appreciate it if you didn't take his seat."

"I'll move when he shows up." Carter swirled his ice for a moment, then checked his watch. "He's really late."

Carter always wore a watch, but this wasn't his sturdy, shock-proof outdoorsman model. This one was sleek and sophisticated—a surprise. His whole appearance was a surprise, actually. She'd never seen him in civilian clothes. Board shorts and a bare chest by the pool didn't count.

He looked just right for Austin after dark. His jeans were so dark, she hadn't realized his pants were denim until just now, when she dropped her gaze to the ribbon in her hand and saw the contrast of his hard thigh against her dress's soft, black chiffon.

She jerked her skirt away. "He'll be here. And when he gets here, I don't want to be seen sitting all cozy with another man."

"This is cozy?" His mocking tone set her teeth on edge. "I'd hate to see your definition of cold."

She couldn't do this. The worry and the hurt were weighing her down. It took effort to keep them from crushing her. She had no energy left to parry Carter's disapproval.

She swallowed down the tears that were so close, too

close, to the surface. They made her voice sound a little rough, and too quiet. "Please. I'm begging you, sit anywhere else in this building, but not on this one bench. Anywhere else. Please."

He stared at her, or glared at her, for a moment. "Okay, fine." He stood.

She was surprised. Relieved. "Thank you. Good night."

Carter walked away to the far end of the long bench, then rounded it and started walking back toward her, toward the stairs. She felt him pass behind her and sighed in relief.

Then he sat down.

On the second bench.

A whole six inches away from her.

I cannot believe this. Controlled, direct communication didn't work with this man. Chloe fell back on the other option. *Ignore him.*

They sat shoulder to shoulder, she facing the window, he facing the theater, in silence. After a moment, she cautiously turned her phone over. Nothing. She looked toward the stairs, but now she had to look around Carter to see them. If Drummer came up those stairs, he'd see Carter first, not her. She wanted Drummer to see a woman with pink and blue flowers in her hair. She touched them lightly, to be sure they were still there, secured in the braided sort of twist she'd spent so much time on this afternoon.

Carter looked toward the stairs with her, then looked back at her and shrugged.

She shot him a dirty look as she felt a loose piece of baby's breath and tucked it back into a braid.

"What's that look for?" Carter asked. "Now what did I do?"

"It's just—if he comes up, I want him to see..." She started to point to her hair, but caught herself and let her hand plop back into her lap.

"You want him to see what? Flowers in your hair? Is that supposed to mean something?"

"Never mind."

"Since when do you wear flowers in your hair? I've never seen you do anything like that."

She rolled her eyes. "You can't wear flowers in uniform."

"Exactly. You don't wear flowers in your hair. Does this guy have any idea that you're an army officer?"

No, she hadn't told Drummer, and she'd been trying to justify that for weeks now, and damn Carter for poking at a sore point. "That is none of your business. Being an army officer has nothing to do with anything."

He snorted, and then he polished off the last of his drink. The ice clinked against the glass as he gestured toward her waist. "This whole pink-ribbon-and-flowers thing isn't the real you. If you present yourself as this sweet girly-girl, he might be a little disappointed when he finds out what you really do for a living. You're looking all sexy tonight, but what's he going to think when you have to leave his bed at dawn for a grenade range?"

And *that* poked at years of insecurity, at all the criticism that serving as a soldier meant she wasn't a normal woman. She hated to hear Carter sounding just like one of those people who made her feel like a freak.

She swept up the long end of the pink ribbon in her hand. "Maybe *this* is the real me, and the camouflage and combat boots are the deception. Maybe I've been deceiving *you*, not him. What if, this whole time, I've been tricking you into thinking I'm a serious army officer—your fellow MP who has your back—when what I really am is a soft 'girly-girl' who loves the ballet and puppies and kittens and sunsets?"

He'd gone very still, staring at her without blinking.

She wasn't going to blink first, that was for damned sure. "What if the real me is a girl who gets a little homesick at her new post, and who gets royally sick of always having to prove that she's qualified for her job despite her gender and her age and anything else that anyone else feels free to criticize, and so she chucks all that competitive crap for a chance to be her real self with a real friend? She wants to spend one evening, just one, with a friend who knows the real her and who likes the real her and who doesn't care what she does for a living or even what her *face* looks like." She leaned forward, leaning into all the hurt. "And that friend, Thane Carter, is definitely not you."

He didn't move. For a few intense seconds, they glared at one another, long enough for her to notice every shade of blue and gray in the irises of his eyes, long enough for her to breathe in an aftershave he didn't wear to work.

He dropped that icy-blue gaze to the pink ribbon in her hand. If she tried, she could imagine that a little sadness touched the angry set of his mouth.

"Yeah. It's not me. I'll see you Monday." He stood and walked away, carrying his glass to the bartender in the corner of the lobby.

Chloe stood, too. Drummer wasn't coming, and sitting alone on a bench wasn't going to change that. She didn't want to go back into the theater, because she didn't need to watch the final scene, where the little girl wakes up to find it was all a dream, and her brave and protective nutcracker prince is nothing more than a broken wooden toy.

Chloe headed for the exit, walking toward the staircase that no one had used to come and find her. The end of the ribbon was still in her hand, so she pulled it, untying the bow, pulling the ribbon free from her waist. As she passed the lobby's large trash can, she raised her hand high and dropped it in.

Chapter Sixteen

"What's that in your hand?"

Ernesto hadn't even made it to his desk, and his fellow platoon sergeant had already zeroed in on the plastic food container he was carrying. "It's a piece of cake. My wife made *tres leches* this weekend."

"Outstanding. Monday mornings need all the help they can get."

"It's not for you, Lloyd." Ernesto tossed his hat on his desk. "The LT was pretty down at PT this morning."

"Yours, too? Carter's all pissed off at the world today. He had high hopes about some girl he was going out with this weekend. I didn't even need to ask if it went bad."

"Michaels was supposed to have a big weekend, too. I did ask. Get this—the guy didn't show."

"He stood her up?" Lloyd whistled low. "Men can be such dumbasses. I know I was, but still—Lieutenant Michaels? I was never *that* dumb."

Ernesto glared at him as he sat.

"I mean, if I were a younger man. And not married. And not an NCO."

"And not in the same company."

"Don't give me your protective-father glare. She's not your teenaged daughter. I can't help it if it's obvious she's got a pretty face."

"She's more than a pretty face. She's smart. She's got her act together. She's the whole package."

"I know that, *Dad*." Lloyd shook his head. "And still, some dumbass stood her up. Men."

"Men." The LT hadn't been in her office yet when he'd walked by. Ernesto kicked back in his chair. "Makes me glad I'm married. I wouldn't want to go through all that garbage again."

"Man, the things I used to do for the sake of a woman. Going to chick flicks. Paying *money* to see chick flicks. Hell, Carter went to a ballet this weekend, poor sucker, and got nothing for his trouble."

"A ballet?"

Lloyd laughed. "Can you believe it?"

Ernesto stopped lounging. "My LT was supposed to have her big date at a ballet this weekend, too. She said it wasn't a total loss, because at least she'd gotten to enjoy the *Nutcracker*."

She'd said it with a shrug and a smile, but Ernesto knew a brave lie when he heard it. His LT hadn't enjoyed anything. She'd been hurt. His wife's cake was the best Ernesto could do for a broken heart.

"Guess that goes to show you the ballet is a sucky place for a date. Hold on." Lloyd sat up. "They both went to a ballet this weekend? And now they're both…?"

They stared at each other. Neither one of them wanted to say it out loud.

"Just a coincidence," Lloyd said.

"Yeah." Ernesto tried to think of a single time the two LTs had shared a laugh or a joke or even a meal in the dining facility. Never, not that he'd seen. "They barely tolerate each other."

"Yeah." Lloyd tapped his desk idly. "But they're both single. Right age for each other. Same kind of attitude. You ever notice that he's got a Mustang and she's got a Charger? I mean, those are competitors but they're both muscle cars. They're both—"

"Stop." Ernesto didn't want his platoon leader anywhere near that kind of trouble. She was a good kid, a real good kid, the kind of LT he hoped would stay and make a career out of it. She wouldn't have much of a career if she got caught fraternizing.

"That would be one hell of a match." Lloyd lowered his voice. "It'd be a hell of a court-martial, too."

"No one's getting court-martialed."

"Letter of reprimand, then."

Ernesto stood and picked up the cake, ready to go find his LT before trouble could find her. "Think about it. Carter went on a date that went south. Michaels didn't go on a date at all. She got stood up." As soon as he said it, he could breathe a little easier.

"That's right, that's right." Lloyd clutched his chest. "Man, that got a little scary. For a minute there, I could kind of see the two of them together."

"They hate each other."

"Right."

"So there's no need to see anything."

"Right."

Ernesto left to go find his LT, anyway.

Dear Drummer,

The cursor blinked. Chloe stared at it, hands poised over her laptop keyboard, waiting for the right words to come to her.

Nothing.

She didn't know what she wanted to accomplish with this letter. She'd been stood up on Saturday and looked at a blank white screen all day Sunday. Today had been one of the hardest Mondays of her life.

I can't stop thinking about you.

She paused. Some cooler, more rational voice said he didn't deserve to know that he'd gotten to her so badly. He shouldn't get to gloat over hurting her feelings. If he was not going to write to her, then she shouldn't write to him, either. Right?

Chloe sighed. She couldn't muster up any anger or

indignation. She didn't have any sense of pride or self-preservation. She just felt empty.

I don't know what made you change your mind. At the theater, I spent the whole time trying to imagine where you could be, but in the end, it doesn't matter. You had your reasons, and they were important to you. I only know you weren't with me, and I missed you.

You must have your reasons for being silent now, too. A blank white screen says it all. This friendship has run its course for you.

"But not for me," she whispered.

You are gone as surely as if a computer glitch had taken you from me without warning. But since it didn't, I have a chance to tell you how much this friendship has meant to me. You've been my stability, my constancy, my anchor while I've been moving from one side of the country to the other. I never told you that, did I? From May to November, I was sent from New York to Georgia to Missouri to Texas. I felt like one of those cartoon hobos with a stick over my shoulder, carrying all my belongings tied up in a red handkerchief. Well, packed in the trunk of my car. My job changed, my coworkers changed, my roommates changed, even the clothes I wear every day changed. My whole life changed, but you were constant. For six months and 2,500 miles, I could stop and open our app and there you would be, friendly words in that friendly blue font, without fail.

Chloe stopped typing to wipe her cheeks. It was okay to shed a few tears. She was inside, not on the balcony where Carter might spot her. Nobody would know that the bold new MP officer in the 584th had spent her Monday night crying over the end of a silly online friendship.

Thank you for keeping me company all these months. Thank you for listening, and for offering good advice—and it was always good advice. I know this, because I didn't follow your advice Saturday night, and things turned out badly.

I couldn't sit next to your empty seat for the second act. I stayed in the lobby, waiting, because I still had the hope that you had only been delayed. I kept checking my phone, though, and that blank white screen was breaking my heart, so I was not ready at all when that friend-who-isn't-really-a-friend walked up to me.

The timing was awful. I should be used to his insults at this point, but when he made fun of my appearance, I kind of snapped. All your advice on controlled confrontations went out the window. I was hurting, and I lashed out at the only person there was to lash out against.

In the moment, it felt like he deserved it. But now, all I can think about is the way he'd walked up to me and said hello, and the way I told him to sit anywhere, anywhere, except next to me.

I want to delete that sentence so that you won't know how awful I can be, but maybe I should leave it in. It was awful of you to stand me up, but it was also awful of me to tell that man I didn't want him near me. I wish I could take it back. If you wish you could take it back, too, then please know that I would still love to talk to you as we always have.

If not, then I'm still glad that, out of all the gin joints in all the towns in all the world, this app sent you walking into mine. I loved being your—

Ballerina Baby.

* * *

Two shorts and a long.

Thane stood on his balcony in the cold December air and glared at Building Four's empty matching balcony. She was over there, just behind those sliding glass doors, and she was trying to reach him. Or rather, she was trying to reach Drummer. He'd promised her he'd be at the theater in D131, and she'd driven an hour to Austin to meet him, and he hadn't shown up. Why would she try to talk to him now? A woman like Michaels would kick a man's ass for standing her up—or at least write him off as a total loss, no longer worthy of her time.

She'd be fine.

She just hadn't been fine yet today. She'd been really quiet, actually. And sad. Her platoon sergeant had seen it. He'd brought her some cake. That was nice; she had someone who'd try to cheer her up in the future. Michaels wasn't friendless, for God's sake, no matter what she'd said so passionately with her pink ribbon in her hand.

She was going to be fine.

Thane looked at his phone. The app's icon indicated one message was waiting. It was probably *screw you and good-bye*. The way she'd walked into row D, down there at orchestra level, so full of hope—she must have been so pissed off when the man had said he wasn't Drummer.

But Thane couldn't fool himself. He'd been able to see her face. She hadn't been pissed off. She'd been sad.

He stared at her empty balcony a moment longer, then he opened the app on his phone. Dear Drummer—

By the time he got to all the gin joints in all the towns, he knew he had to write her at least one more time.

Casablanca. (Too easy.) I wish I had an easy explanation about Saturday. I do not. But I want you to know that you did nothing wrong. If I could have made everything turn out differently, I would have.

Thane did not hit Send.

He'd wanted everything to turn out differently, it was true, for every selfish reason. In his perfect scenario, he would have walked into row D and found a woman who was beautiful, easy to talk to, quick to smile, interesting to him, interested in him. He'd experienced that only once before in his life, with Chloe, stunning Chloe, with whom he'd damned near fallen in love at first sight.

He'd wanted a new woman to be as exciting as Chloe. He'd wanted lightning to strike twice.

Only now, on a miserable, lonely Monday evening, could he admit to himself how much he still missed Chloe and the dream of what might have been. The reality was that, from the first moment of that first ride-along, Chloe had never acted like a woman who'd missed the dream of being with him. In the parking lot of the MP station, rather than being shocked or hurt or sad when she'd seen him, she'd taken him to task. Chloe had turned into Michaels within a few sentences, and he'd been resenting her ever since.

Ah, hell. The truth hit him in the face. Michaels was Ballerina, so the friend-who-wasn't-a-friend was him. She'd confronted him in the parking lot because that's what *he* had advised her to do.

He looked once more at her sliding glass doors. All along, he'd been the coworker who made her professional life hell. As Drummer, he'd been so worried that the not-a-friend would hurt her…

And he had, a low blow when she'd least expected it, on a Saturday night when she'd been all dressed up for her favorite ballet. Thane closed his eyes against the memory of the hope on her face every time she'd turn to look at that mezzanine staircase.

He slunk back into his apartment, slid the door shut and leaned against his wall. He looked at his phone once more, and felt all the truth of his blue words. I want you to know that you did nothing wrong.

She wasn't going to believe him. Her letter was too full of apology, telling him she was sometimes a bad person, too, offering him an easy olive branch.

She should have told him to go to hell. She'd done nothing wrong at the theater, and he'd stood her up. One month ago, she'd done nothing wrong by the pool, and he'd left her without an explanation. She'd done nothing wrong by requesting a radio on their first ride-along. She'd done nothing wrong by developing a better duty officer schedule. She'd done nothing wrong.

But he had.

He slid down the wall, wishing he could start over. That was impossible, but if he could tell Chloe everything and ask for a second chance—but that would be fraternization. Lieutenant Thane Carter couldn't open his heart to her.

Drummer could. As long as Chloe never found out that Drummer was him, she would be safe from any fraternization charges. She would be completely innocent.

He wouldn't be, but it was a risk he needed to take. He needed to be Drummer for her, just for a little bit longer, so Ballerina wouldn't be left so abruptly alone.

At the same time, Thane Carter could start being a better friend to Chloe Michaels. He couldn't court her. He couldn't date her, but he could be her friend. Maybe, once she had that real-life friend she wanted so badly, she would say goodbye to Drummer on her own terms. She'd be free to find a new man to love.

It wouldn't be him. He could only be her friend.

If I could have made everything turn out differently, I would have.

Thane hit Send.

Chapter Seventeen

Christmas Eve at the brigade's dining facility was a come one, come all feast for the soldiers who stayed in the Fort Hood area during the holidays. Soldiers with their spouses and children, their parents and a few sets of grandparents, would shortly begin making their way through the cafeteria-style line of food stations for an old-fashioned turkey dinner with all the trimmings.

It was traditional for the officers to dress in the service uniform, the formal dark blue suit with rank and regalia displayed to precise standards. They showed up with medals on their chests and spit-shined shoes, and then were sent behind the food line like school cafeteria workers to serve the holiday meal to their troops.

Thane had always enjoyed it. As an eighteen-year-old private, he'd gotten a kick out of having a full-bird colonel scoop mashed potatoes onto his plate. As a twenty-six-year-old officer, he got a kick out of watching his soldiers interact with their children. It was priceless to hear the toughest, most battle-hardened sergeants say things like *It's not polite to put your fingers in your sister's nose at the table*.

Thane had already taken his holiday leave at Thanksgiving, weeks before the *Nutcracker* debacle. He'd driven to South Carolina, seen his folks, hit the old bars, and affirmed that the gulf between himself and the friends he'd left behind when he'd joined the army was still there.

Christmas would be spent here. Thane looked for the mess hall sergeant, ready for his assignment to scoop sweet potatoes or ladle gravy. The battalion commander would be carving the turkey. The CO of the 410th was already posted by the trays of green bean casserole, and standing over there, next to the pumpkin pies, was Michaels.

Chloe.

Thane devoured her for a hot second with his eyes. She wore the crossed pistols of the Military Police Corps on her lapels, the gold embroidery of her rank on her shoulder boards, silver wings on her chest for Airborne and Air Assault qualifications. Lieutenant Chloe Michaels in her dress blues should be on a recruitment poster. Young girls would aspire to be her. Parents would want their daughters to turn out like her. What man wouldn't admire her?

He did.

The mess sergeant saved Thane from his own thoughts by handing him a pair of tongs and sending him over to a giant basket of rolls. Bread was the last station before the dessert table. He'd have to stare at Michaels's back the whole time. Great.

Actually, it *was* great. Michaels's uniform was perfectly tailored to her trim waist. Her skirt was hemmed to fall precisely at the middle of her knee. Her legs weren't nude like last Saturday, but smooth with the polish of panty hose. Her black pumps weren't stilettos, but they were high-heeled. She wasn't dressing like a sexy girlfriend, but a professional officer in a uniform that carried both authority and history.

She looked sexy, anyway.

Music came on the loudspeakers, families came through the doors.

"Merry Christmas, sir."

"You, too, Sergeant First Class. You want the pretzel roll or the sourdough?"

Passing out rolls didn't stop him from thinking about Chloe. No wonder the girls in his hometown bars hadn't held any appeal for him at Thanksgiving. He'd looked. He'd wanted someone to knock him out. Plenty of pretty women had talked to him. Even the most distant acquaintance greeted him with a hug and a kiss on the cheek, soft hands on his chest, his neck, his biceps. Everyone had smiled, but no one had been intriguing enough to invite out to dinner, no one had made him want to go somewhere quieter to get to know her. Thane had given up looking for more, and had tried to enjoy the flirting for what it was.

It wasn't much. He'd left the bar and gone to his parents' house, so he could type on the phone with Ballerina instead. He'd wanted her to be that real-life friend more than ever, but she could've lived a thousand miles away, for all he'd known at Thanksgiving. Now, on Christmas Eve, he knew Ballerina was here.

For two hours, he watched her give children extra whipped cream. For two hours, he felt his heart break. The most he could hope for with that amazing woman was the friend zone. Hell, he needed to dig himself out of a hole just to *get* to the friend zone.

It was time to start digging.

When the dinner was over and only the cooks and a few officers were left, Thane filled a plate with everything except a roll and took a seat across from Michaels.

She nodded to acknowledge him, nothing like the girls at the bars back home. No smile. No words. No touch.

He wanted that touch. He couldn't have it, but the desire scrambled his brain. It was hard to speak casually to her. *Ballerina, it's me...*

It's me, the guy who stood you up.

"What are you doing tomorrow for Christmas, Chloe?"

She gave him an odd look. "I'm the duty officer, *Thane*."

Ah, he'd slipped and called her Chloe, thus the odd look.

"How did you get stuck with duty on Christmas Day?" Just two days ago, she'd left their office and gone home at 1100 hours after pulling duty. She shouldn't be the MPDO for another eight nights.

"I volunteered."

"For Christmas? You didn't take leave on Thanksgiving, either, right?"

"Right. I didn't." She was so formal in her formal uniform, but she was distant with him in combat boots, too.

They ought to be closer, like teammates. They ought to at least be on a first-name basis.

"Chloe."

"Thane."

He almost smiled as she imitated him. If she only knew how much he liked hearing her say his name…

"Chloe, you don't have to deprive yourself of a chance to see your family. There will be plenty of times in your career when you won't have any choice about working a holiday. You'll be working a flood or an ice storm or something else you can't control, or you'll be stationed halfway around the world in a hostile environment. When you're stateside, it's expected that you'll take at least one of the winter holidays off. It's not wimping out to go see your family."

She looked at him with a little wrinkle of concern between her eyebrows.

"Unless you aren't close to your family?" Thane asked. "Did I bring up a sore subject?"

"I get along fine with my family."

Of course she did. He'd never heard Ballerina complain about family drama.

"Then be sure to go home now and then. When you decide to go, let me know." Thane decided to be the first to smile. "I'll give you a ride to the airport."

Her eyes opened wide. Damn, was that something he'd talked about with Ballerina or with Chloe?

Sergeant Gevahr, the squad leader who lived at Two Rivers, passed their table, wishing them both a happy holiday with his civilian girlfriend. Chloe smiled and gave him a little wave goodbye. She returned her attention to Thane, and her smile faded away to that formal nothingness.

He needed to fix this relationship. It wasn't acceptable to him anymore that her smile died when he was around.

"Why did you volunteer to work Christmas?"

"I designed that schedule. You and Salvatore and Phillips

got stuck with extra shifts this month because of it. I wasn't going to let you miss Christmas, too."

"It was an extra three shifts for each of us in the whole month of December. Big deal. Don't sit there feeling guilty. Tomorrow should have fallen on one of the 410th guys, anyway. It was their month to pull duty before the new schedule, so they were already expecting it. You didn't need to take one for them."

She tilted her head and studied him. "What is this about, Carter? Are you giving me advice? Are you *mentoring* me now?"

"Believe it or not, I'm not always a jerk. Try me. What's going on?"

"Nothing."

"Something." He pushed the salt and pepper toward her when she reached for it.

"Nothing, and I want to keep it that way. I don't want anyone to have cause for complaint about a schedule that was my idea."

"It might have been your idea, but it was the battalion commander's decision. If anyone gripes about it, tell him to take it up with Colonel Stephens."

She only sighed and moved on to her dessert.

"Has someone said something to you?"

"Of course not." She cut through her pumpkin pie with the side of her fork, making a sharp little clink of sound on the sturdy plate. "No one will gripe about the new schedule to my face. That's too easy to deal with. I'm trying to make sure no one has a reason to sneer at me behind my back. How dare that new female officer come in here and change the way we've always done it?"

Thane said nothing. It was too close to what he'd thought himself.

"In every assignment, I walk in with two strikes against me, and I know it. I'm female and a West Pointer. I have to prove I'm… I don't know. Normal, for starters. Then worthy of the rank on my shoulders."

Again, it was too close to true. Before she'd even made it to the unit, Lloyd had taken great glee in announcing Thane's new office mate was going to be a West Pointer and a girl to boot. The comment had seemed harmless, even routine, but today, over a piece of pumpkin pie, Thane realized that he and everyone else had indeed been reserving judgment.

She'd proved herself to everyone during their first ride-along—everyone in the 584th. When she'd been the duty officer this month, she'd probably had to prove herself all over again to the soldiers of the 410th. They must have been judging her every move far more than they had with him or Phillips or Salvatore. When she joined a unit, she had to prove herself upon arrival. When Thane joined a new unit, he was assumed to be competent unless he proved otherwise. Subtle difference, but it was a real difference.

Chloe shrugged like they'd been talking about the weather as she ate her dessert. "Anyway, if I just take the Christmas shift myself, that removes one more thing someone might gripe about when I'm not around. So far, the dynamics in our battalion seem to be good, at least to my face. I'd like to keep it that way. Pulling duty is like a Christmas present from me, to me. I've given myself one less thing to worry about." She finished her pie and tossed her napkin onto her tray. "Well, you have a nice Christmas—"

"Chloe."

"Thane."

"The dynamics are going well behind your back, too, not just to your face. I'm in the boys' club by default. I would've heard any negative comments about you. There aren't any." Thane pushed his plate out of the way and leaned forward, resting his forearms on the table. "If anyone did something idiotic, like blame you when they pulled a bad duty officer shift, I'd set them straight right then and there."

After a long moment, she stood. With tray in hand, she nodded at Thane.

"Same."

Then she walked away.

How was your day?

Chloe stretched out on her sofa with her laptop on her stomach. It was noon on the twenty-sixth of December, and she'd just gotten home after being the Christmas MPDO. Drummer had left this question for her on the app, probably expecting her to read it after a normal workday at five or six o'clock. She'd leave him an answer and then go to sleep.

It was really slow and boring, since it was Christmas. I had a nice Christmas Eve dinner with my coworkers, though. It ended a little weirdly. Mr. Not-a-Friend made an appearance.

And?

Chloe lifted her hands from the keyboard in surprise at the blue And? She hadn't expected Drummer to be online. His icon hadn't been flashing when she'd logged on.

And he was mostly ok.

Mostly?

Thane had been more than okay. He'd looked far too handsome in dress blues, which had made her as uncomfortable as seeing him in civilian clothes at the *Nutcracker*. She preferred Thane in baggy camouflage. In dress blues or in denim, or definitely in a bathing suit with a bare chest, Thane was too attractive to ignore.

He never seemed to be attracted to her, but he had tried to share a meal and a conversation, which was weird in itself.

Mostly. I had to educate him a little on boys vs. girls. I get so tired of boys vs. girls in my job. He told me how I should act toward the other guys, but it's how he would act. It's a different minefield for girls, but not a lot of men get that. The boys always assume they are the standard. There's a certain arrogance in being sure your way will work.

He's arrogant? Could it be anything else? Is he older than you are? Is he more senior in your career field?

Chloe froze with her hands over the keyboard—again. How did Drummer do that? Since the very beginning of their relationship, he'd always been so insightful despite the limited details they gave each other.

Yes, he's both. He likes to lord that over me. But lately, he's actually been helpful on occasion. He's not hard to work with.

That's good. You're making progress with him, then.

Progress? Chloe hadn't been trying to do anything except avoid him.

This is the same guy that we had to come up with options for. Controlled confrontation and all that. I guess that was the right way to handle him, since he's being nicer now. That's good, because my job requires a lot of teamwork.

Teamwork. What do you do for a living again?

* * *

Across the parking lot, in Building Six, Thane waited for her reply.

If she'd just break the boundaries they'd set and say she was in the military, then he could say he was in the military, too. He could direct the conversation naturally from there. They were both in the military, both in the Austin area. It would be obvious to conclude they were both at Fort Hood.

They would agree to meet, and this time, he'd sit beside her, wherever it was. He would pretend that he was just as surprised as she was. Surprised, but not entirely shocked, because they would have already been expecting to meet a fellow army officer. Just not each other.

But once she realized he'd been her online love for more than half a year, he'd sweep her off her feet in real life. He'd wrap his arms around her, something more sensual than the hug that every other friend gave her. He'd savor the warmth and weight of her body in his arms. He'd pull all the pins out of that ballerina bun and let her hair cascade to her shoulders. He'd bury his hands in it, he'd look into her brown eyes as he traced the curves and lines of her face with his fingertips, and he'd finally, finally taste her lips, just like he did in his dreams.

The cursor blinked at him.

He willed her to answer him, just a few words: *I bet you'd never guess this, but I'm in the military.* That was all she had to say. He would take it from there.

His dreams were unrealistic—and against regulations—but meeting in real life would be a good start. The kiss would have to wait, but their fragile friendship would become solid. Someday, they would no longer serve in the same unit, and once that day came, he would woo her, court her, pursue her with all the emotion he currently had to keep tightly leashed. If she would just give him the opening, just tell him she was in the military…

That wasn't very subtle, Drummer. We've done pretty well by keeping our careers a secret since last June. I don't want to change that now.

"Damn it." He pushed to his feet and paced the width of his apartment. Chloe was so by the book. Such a little rule follower.

Her next words cooled his frustration before it could pick up steam: If we'd met at the theater last week, we would know each other's careers and a lot more right now. Maybe it would have been better, but then again, maybe not. Maybe we wouldn't even be friends anymore. But without having met and without knowing the details of our lives, we are definitely still friends. Let's not mess with what works.

He had blown it, not her. Thane had walked away from her at a pool party. Drummer had stood her up at a theater. Why should she trust him in either of his personas again?

Can we talk later, Drummer? I just got home from my job, and I really need to get some sleep. But I really need to have some fun after that. Will you be around?

He never wanted to hurt her again. He couldn't refuse to be there if she needed his company, so he kept up the charade. I'll be around. Get some rest. If you haven't got your health, you haven't got anything.

It took her less than a second. (The Princess Bride! You finally quoted the Princess Bride!) I'm only going to sleep for a couple of hours, because I don't want to get my days and nights mixed up. Let's do dinner and a movie. You pick the movie and tell me what channel, okay?

There was only one possible answer: As you wish, Baby. As you wish.

Chapter Eighteen

Six weeks.

It had been six weeks since Thane had found out who Ballerina really was. Six weeks since he'd started being a real-life friend to Chloe, so she wouldn't need her virtual friend, and she'd let Drummer go.

No luck.

Drummer still enjoyed talking to Ballerina too much. He meant to dial back his engagement with her as Drummer and let Thane fill in the gap, but then they'd start typing back and forth about which movie was the most quotable—he said *The Godfather*, she said *The Princess Bride*, but they used *Casablanca* the most—and next thing he knew, he'd spent another entire evening online with his best friend.

Six weeks. The clock was ticking. He'd gotten some firm dates through the S-1 today. He was going to be promoted to captain in May. Then he'd be sent to the captain's course at Fort Leonard Wood in June, a six-month school. That would be followed by an assignment as a company commander.

Unless he blew it before then. He'd have to do something really stupid, like drunk driving. Like disobeying a regulation—like fraternization.

Four months. He had four months before he could tell Chloe how he felt, legally. Four months until he could apologize for things she didn't know he'd done. Four months before he could try to turn friends into lovers while he lived in Missouri and she in Texas.

There would be no long-distance romance without having that friendship first. He needed to get rid of Drummer.

No time like the present.

They were at their desks. Thane sat back and typed a line to Ballerina on his phone, a casual blue hello. He hit Send.

Chloe's phone buzzed a second later. He watched her concentrating on her government-issued laptop, typing away diligently at some necessary bit of administrative work. She glanced at her phone. Kept typing.

Thane sent Ballerina another line. Are you busy?

Another buzz. Another quick glance.

Thane really shouldn't enjoy teasing her this much. One more message. This time he stood up as he hit Send.

Her phone buzzed.

"Yo, Chloe. Your phone is blowing up. Got a secret admirer?"

She glared at him, but she picked up her phone. Thane stepped around his desk as she opened a very familiar white screen with pink and blue writing.

"Who's bugging you?" he asked.

"None of your business."

"You're not still exchanging sweet nothings with the creep who stood you up at the *Nutcracker*, are you?"

She typed a word, maybe two on her phone, and hit Send.

His phone didn't buzz; he'd set it on silent. He crossed his arms over his chest and leaned against her desk, half sitting on the corner. "You are."

"I am not."

"You're almost blushing. Lieutenant Chloe Michaels isn't the blushing type. You wouldn't be lying, would you?"

She set her phone on her desk, screen side down, and sat back in her chair, crossing her arms like his. "I never type sweet nothings. He and I discuss things that matter. Conversations I wouldn't expect you to understand."

Thane bit his tongue. Hard. They conversed about vampire kindergartens and cold fried chicken. They rated the hotness factor of the 1960s aliens that appeared on the original *Star Trek*. "Why would you do that? Why should you discuss anything with him, sweet or not, when he stood you up?"

"He couldn't make it."

"That was December. It's February. It's been two months. Has he tried to set anything up that he *could* make?"

"It's February first. It's only been six weeks."

"I'll take that as a *no*. Aren't you bothered that he hasn't tried to see you again?" *Come on, Chloe, dump the guy*.

"We enjoy talking to each other. We talk for hours. We don't need to meet in person to do that."

He needed to try a new tactic. He'd been so frustrated when he'd wanted to meet Ballerina and she'd said no. Maybe if he could get her to want to meet Drummer and then Drummer said no...

"Why don't you take the first step? Maybe he's embarrassed about being a no-show last time. Maybe he'd be relieved if you gave him a second chance. Invite him to a movie or something."

"If he wanted to catch a movie, he's man enough to say so."

"I'm telling you, he's waiting for you to make the first move. I'm a guy. Guys know how guys think."

She tilted her head and studied him a moment. "How about your date at the ballet? Are you two still hot and heavy?"

"I never claimed we were hot and heavy, but I like how your imagination works."

"I'm not using my imagination. It's observation. You weren't dressed like a man who was expecting an intellectual date with his platonic friend."

Thane had to smile at that. Chloe had liked the way he looked that night, apparently. "Don't you think a woman would be pretty mad if I missed the second act to drink whiskey with you?"

"With me? You told her you were with me?" Her tone of voice made it sound like an utter impossibility. "Tell her not to worry."

"It's hard to tell a woman not to worry if I spend the evening enjoying a whiskey and conversation with a woman in a low-cut black dress."

She blinked—but she recovered quickly. "You were enjoying yourself? Hardly."

"Don't sell yourself short. It's not that hard to enjoy a conversation with you."

She looked at him like he was absolutely insane. Damn, they had a long way to go.

"Come on. I'll prove it to you. Let's go get lunch."

"Where?" She was always suspicious when he was nice to her.

"The dining facility's serving hot dogs and tater tots today. I remember that you like your dogs naked, but how do you dress your tots?"

She looked away from him. He'd noticed before that she didn't like to be reminded about their first day at the pool.

He didn't back off. "It's like your hot dog test. I'll learn all about your personality. Come on, Chloe. I'm starving."

"Fine."

Success. When she stood up and grabbed her patrol cap, he had to work to stay cool about it. They walked out of the headquarters building together. Like associates. Like fellow platoon leaders in the same unit. Like friends.

"Let me guess," he said, feeling jubilant that he had her by his side. "With everything I know about you, I predict that you'll put ketchup on half of your tots, mustard on the other half, and salt the heck out of everything."

"What—how—" She looked shocked at his guess.

"Not a hard guess. You're a pretty salty woman. Must come from somewhere."

They walked a little farther in silence—and in step. Thane wondered if that was just a military thing, or if he and Chloe were tuned in to each other.

"Tater tots don't reveal a thing about a person," she said stiffly, still in sync.

"Then you've got nothing to fear. We can safely enjoy lunch and still not accidentally like each other."

"No chance of that."

"Really?" He'd said that wrong. He sounded a little, just a little, wistful. But she hadn't sounded as convinced as she usually did, either. "Really, Chloe? There's no chance that we might like each other?"

"What do you mean?"

It wasn't time to reveal everything. It might never be time to reveal everything, but he could at least tell her part of the truth.

"Do you ever think—"

Two privates walked toward them on the sidewalk. They saluted. "Good afternoon, sir. Good afternoon, ma'am."

He and Chloe returned their salutes.

"Do I ever think what?" Chloe asked. At least he had her curious enough to continue the subject.

"Do you ever wonder how we would have gotten along if the first time we'd met had been at work instead of at that pool?"

"No." Chloe looked away, predictably. He'd mentioned the pool.

Another private came toward them on the sidewalk, a sergeant close behind her. The closer they got to the dining facility, the more salutes had to be given and returned.

Thane waited a moment for the soldiers to get a little distance away. "I wonder about it. If the first time I'd met you had been at the station, if the watch commander had introduced you as the new platoon leader, I would've been more open-minded. I would have given you a chance instead of arguing before we even got in the car."

"Oh." She wouldn't look at him.

He couldn't keep his eyes off her. "I would have been impressed with you by the end of that shift, Chloe. You've got the right attitude. You've got common sense. I would have felt like the 584th had won the lottery when it came to new lieutenants."

"As opposed to what? Since that didn't happen, you don't think I'm a lottery prize?"

"As opposed to the way I acted. I acted like I wasn't impressed, but I was. I should have been a better mentor from the very first night, instead of—"

Another soldier jogged toward them in a rush, slowed to a walk, saluted. "Afternoon, sir, afternoon, ma'am." Started jogging again.

"Better?" Chloe asked. "You haven't been any kind of mentor at all."

"I know." They were getting close to the dining facility, so they'd be running a gauntlet of military courtesy in a moment. He had to speak now or hold his peace. "I'm glad you've had Sergeant Ernesto. He won't steer you wrong. But I've given up being an ass, Chloe. It's too hard to sustain it around a person who doesn't deserve it. Who never deserved it. If Ernesto's not around and you need anything—"

They both greeted the major who came out of the dining facility and saluted him. Thane stopped just before the door. "Before we go in…"

"What?" She looked a little apprehensive.

He didn't want to freak her out. It was time to lighten up. "Before we go in, let's hear your guess on the tater tots. How do you think I take them?"

"You're weird."

He smiled. That was almost a term of affection between Drummer and Ballerina. "Take a guess."

"I think it's a trick question. I think you choose french fries."

He laughed, genuinely surprised. "You're right. You're one hundred percent right. How'd you guess that?"

"You take your hot dogs all fancy-schmanzy. You probably take your side item plain. For balance."

"Balance. You take your hot dog plain, and your tots fancy. Between the two of us, we've got all the bases covered. I told you, we might turn out to be friends."

"Heard you had quite the night, sir."

Chloe hung up her desk phone and looked at her platoon

sergeant. He'd come into her office, two steps behind Thane, but apparently not to talk to her.

Thane sat, slowly, heavily, like his body was weighing him down. The chair wheels squeaked loudly. He half-heartedly raised an eyebrow at her, but barely returned her grin.

They had a running joke about that squeaky chair. Last week, they'd sneaked it into Lloyd's office and taken his. Like a game of hot potato, Lloyd had traded it out for one in the orderly room. Yesterday, the chair had made its way back to Chloe, so she'd switched it with Thane's while he was on duty. He should have grinned at the squeak and started planning where to dump the chair next, but instead he was rubbing his forehead like a man who was even more exhausted than a twenty-four-hour shift normally made a person.

"You should go home now, sir."

Thane had no grin at all for Ernesto. "I'm fine, Sergeant First Class. I know Lloyd's out for the week, but you don't have to take over his mother-hen duties. I'll go home when my work is done."

Ernesto shook off his XO's words. "There's nothing critical on the schedule today, sir. No reason to not go home."

Thane pulled a clipboard out of a drawer and slapped it down on his desk. "This fire marshal thing is due. Today. Regulation requires an officer to do it. I appreciate your concern, Sergeant First Class, but if I say I'm fine, I'm fine. I'll go home when I'm ready."

For the last two weeks, ever since Thane had buried the hatchet over hot dogs and tater tots, they'd been conspiring together to come up with practical jokes and laughing nearly every day. This morning, Thane did not look like a man who had laughed in a year.

Chloe had no idea what was going on, but she trusted Ernesto. If he thought Thane should go home, then Thane should go. No one could make him go except the CO. She checked her watch. The CO wouldn't be out of his battalion staff meeting for a couple of hours.

Thane looked more than tired. More than angry. Something was wrong.

"I can do the fire marshal duty," she said.

"No."

"Why not? What's involved?"

He sighed as if she'd asked a difficult question. "You check the gauge of every fire extinguisher in every building and initial that each one is charged."

"I can certainly see why they need a commissioned officer for that." What a typical army thing, to require an officer's legal authority for such a simple task. She would have laughed if Thane didn't look so angry.

Concern and kindness from Ernesto were only making him bristle. She'd have to try something else.

She stood and picked up the clipboard. "Do you think I can't handle this? You're not that special, Thane. My initials are just as legal as your initials."

"It has to be at the S-3 by noon. The brigade S-3, not the battalion S-3."

"Ooh, scary." She wiggled the fingers of one hand like something was spooky—her right hand, just to annoy him with her ring. Then she smacked him lightly on the shoulder with the clipboard. "I can handle this, Thane. You look like hell. Go home."

She left before he could argue with her or try to take the clipboard back. On her way out, she exchanged a quick glance with Ernesto.

Make him go.

Chapter Nineteen

Assist-protect-defend.

Thane couldn't get the motto out of his damned head. It pounded in his brain as he pounded up the concrete steps toward his apartment.

He'd taken such pride in his profession. Assist, protect, defend—it sounded so selfless, so noble. He'd helped a lot of people in the past two years. Each one had made him more confident that he'd be able to help the next one. A kind of arrogance had built, unchecked, because he had always been able to help the next one.

Until now.

The accident scene had been a nightmare. A single car upside down on an empty country road, its deflated airbag hanging out a shattered window, headlights still on and beaming into the night, illuminating the unmistakable mass that was a human being in the middle of the road.

Thane had been calling it in on the radio as he'd driven closer, when his own headlights had shone on a second body in the road. He'd slammed on his brakes so that he wouldn't hit it. Her.

He'd thrown his car in Park and gotten out, but as he'd dropped to his knees by the woman in his headlights, he'd spotted the third body on the shoulder of the road.

Assist, protect, defend—which one?

For one hideous second, he'd knelt there, paralyzed. Where could he even begin? What help could he possibly be? He was insignificant in the face of real laws—of physics, of biology. Force and velocity defeated skin and bone, and the badge on his vest didn't mean he could change the laws for these three people. *Here we all are, gathered together in these headlights. Helpless.*

One frozen second—and then all his years of training had

kicked in, and he'd given all he had to the woman under his hands. There'd been no pulse. There'd been a lot of blood. He'd forced breath into her lungs, tied a tourniquet between exhales.

The woman on the shoulder had regained consciousness, moaning in pain for long moments, then gaining enough strength to cry out for help. As he'd worked on her friend, Thane had assisted her using the only thing he had left: his voice. *I'm here. Help's coming. Hold on. Hold on.* Short sentences were all he'd been able to manage as he'd kept breathing for the woman who'd lost so much blood.

She'd begun breathing on her own by the time they loaded her into the back of the ambulance. The conscious woman had been loaded into the next ambulance. Paramedics had clustered around the third woman, the one so far down the road, his headlights hadn't touched her. The medics had done their job while he'd done his, directing MPs to secure the scene until the traffic investigators could arrive with their tape measures and cameras.

The ambulances had screamed away, sirens fading as they took the broken bodies and left the broken car. Traffic would do their analysis and arrange the tow truck. Thane's part was over; 310 was free to go.

He'd gotten a lot of pats on the back, approving touches that told him he'd been a success. Success had been bloody. He'd needed to clean up, so he'd gotten into his patrol car and headed back to the station. When the watch commander had brought him a cup of coffee, Thane had known he looked as rough outside as he felt inside.

But soap and water and a cup of coffee did a lot for a man. The relief that the woman hadn't died under his hands had turned to a strange sense of euphoria, but it hadn't lasted long enough. Anger had set in by the time he'd left the station and gone to his office.

Anger that he still felt as he pounded up the stairs. Anger at himself for that second of paralysis. Anger that he'd had his blissfully ignorant arrogance stripped away from him in a frozen moment on the blacktop. He'd never again be able to take life for granted the way he had before he'd knelt on the road.

Life was vulnerable. Life could not defy physics, and yet, Thane passed door after door where full lives were lived. He was surrounded by life. He had a life.

It was so incredibly valuable. What should he spend it on? Happiness.

Ballerina's goal. He'd asked her what her goal in life was, big life, but he'd never stopped to ask himself the same thing.

Thane reached the top of the stairs. Before he pulled out his apartment key, he pulled out his phone. He wanted to talk through everything with Ballerina, but her real name was Chloe, and he knew she was currently counting fire extinguishers.

She was counting those fire extinguishers for him, because she cared about him. Somehow, by some miracle, she cared about him.

That was so incredibly valuable. Caring for another person, loving another person, that should be his priority in life. He loved her. He'd loved her since the first marathon typing session with Ballerina, eight months ago.

He put his phone away and walked into his apartment, alone.

Never delay happiness. He'd heard that before, but now he felt the urgency.

Never delay happiness—but he couldn't even try to find happiness with Chloe until June, when they would be a thousand miles apart.

The anger came back and choked him.

When Chloe got back to her office, Ernesto was waiting.

"Word came from the hospital, ma'am."

"Who is in the hospital?" she asked calmly. Her gut

churned. Had Thane been more than tired? Had she walked out of here and left a critically ill man behind?

"Lieutenant Carter worked an accident scene last night. The LT was first on the scene. Word is that he was the only one on the scene for a while. It happened out on a range road, so it took the ambulance a little extra time to get there. Three victims. Single-car rollover. All of them were ejected from the vehicle."

Chloe crossed her arms over her chest, but no layers, not arms, not jackets, not shirts, could protect her heart from feeling pain. No wonder Thane had looked so rough.

"How many fatalities?" Times like these, she knew she wasn't normal. She was able to stand in the face of terrible news and function with a clear mind. Not a normal response, but a necessary one.

"Lieutenant Carter did CPR on one woman. She's in the ICU, but she's still alive. One was conscious when they brought her in. She's going to make it for sure, they say. The third one got thrown the farthest from the wreck. She passed away about half an hour ago. I thought maybe you or the CO would want to stop by Lieutenant Carter's this evening to update him."

The flag wouldn't go down for another six hours. Thane should be sound asleep right now, but she didn't like the idea of him being alone for the next six hours if he wasn't.

"I'll go now. Put me down as LOP on your way through the orderly room, please."

"You got it, ma'am."

LOP stood for *Lost on Post*. It meant that, while somebody was not quite skipping work, it was best not to track whatever they were doing too closely. If the CO wanted to know more, he would ask her. Everyone else would just accept that the LT was out on a task of personal importance.

Thane Carter was of personal importance to her. She just didn't want to analyze why. It was just true.

* * *

"Come on, Thane. I know you're not asleep. I saw you sitting on your balcony."

Thane looked through the peephole. Chloe was standing there in her ACUs, but she didn't look happy to be there.

He didn't want her to be there, either. This was not a good time for him to have to pretend that he saw her as just his teammate. Just a friend.

"Shouldn't you be at work?" he hollered through the door.

"Shouldn't you be asleep?" she hollered back.

He sighed and opened the door, but he left the chain in place, keeping her out as if she might be dangerous.

She was. Dangerous and terribly beautiful.

She held up a handful of napkin-wrapped circles. "I had to confiscate some cookies before the dining facility opened as part of my fire inspection. Chocolate chip today."

He stuck his arm through the gap, palm up. "Thanks."

She held them just out of his reach. "Come on. Invite me in. I've never seen your place." The smile on her face was hopeful.

He'd killed that hopeful smile at the *Nutcracker*. He probably couldn't live with himself if he killed it again.

Thane pulled his arm back in, shut the door to take off the chain, then stepped back and let her in. She took off her patrol cap and handed him the cookies. And crumbs. They spilled out of the napkins onto his floor. He brushed some off the plain T-shirt he'd put on after his shower. She walked right past him, looking at his place with blatant curiosity.

"Does it pass inspection?" he asked drily, still standing by the open door.

She turned around, smiling like she was pleased with herself for having gotten past his attempt to keep her out. "I think you could possibly get a larger TV in here, maybe an inch larger, if you really tried. What is it with guys and giant TVs?"

He shut the front door. "Out with it, Chloe. The cookies are nice. What's really going on?"

She sighed and sat on his couch. "I've got news. From the hospital."

"Go ahead."

She gave it to him straight, all facts, no speculation, no emotion. Any other way would have driven him crazy.

"At least the lady I worked on is hanging on."

Since Chloe seemed in no rush to leave, Thane sat down, too—in the recliner. He was not going to cozy up on the couch with Chloe.

"You did well," she said.

He just looked at her, a real-life friend, sharing his space. It was so unremarkable. It was the reason for living.

"So eat a cookie." She winked at him, then picked up his remote and flopped back on the couch cushions. She found the on button quickly. "Dang, look at the picture on this thing. It's like being in a movie theater."

"Aren't you supposed to be at work?" The cookie tasted like manna. She must have stolen it fresh out of the industrial oven.

"Aren't you supposed to be sleeping?"

"If you leave, I'll sleep."

She used the remote to gesture at the recliner. "If you fall asleep, I'll leave."

She started scrolling through one hundred channels, making him smile at her wisecracks about what made each show unwatchable. It was like having Ballerina on audio instead of in writing. Thane pushed his seatback back, letting the recliner do its recliner thing.

And then he woke up. The TV was still on, and when he turned his head, he saw Chloe was still on the couch. She'd taken off her ACU jacket and was lounging back in the plain brown uniform T-shirt, legs still hidden by camouflage, her booted feet resting on his coffee table.

"You didn't leave."

"It's one heck of a TV. Besides, I've got to see which of the three houses these yahoos choose—oh! I knew it. Idiots." She tore her eyes from the screen and looked at him. "Why would you pass on the French château with the mountain view that was *in budget*? Why? Who does that?"

"Watching TV is pretty stressful for you, isn't it?"

"Yeah. I'm going to go back to work, where life is easy." She stood and stretched, arms high over her head as she yawned.

Chloe in a bikini, standing less than an arm's length away, dropping the towel, moving her chair into the sun. The lust hit Thane hard. Lust for Chloe. Lust for life.

Never delay happiness. But he had four months until June. Four months until he'd be far, far away, trying to capture happiness by asking her to be more than a friend over the phone. Asking her to wait for him, for six months while he took the captain's course. A company command after that, anywhere the army wanted him to go, perhaps another hardship tour in Korea. Hardship tours meant no family members were stationed with the soldier. He gave the army credit for understanding what a hardship was.

Chloe deserved better.

She was oblivious to his thoughts as she put her ACU jacket back on and zipped it up. Thane stood, too, and moved to the door with her.

"This was fun. We should do it again sometime." She picked up her patrol cap. "I'll come over next time *Pride and Prejudice* is on. Mr. Darcy will be life-size on that screen."

He couldn't laugh with her. Her smiles were killing him. She was everything he wanted, and everything he couldn't have.

"Anytime," he said, anyway.

"Great. I gained a friend and a TV. Why didn't we become friends sooner?"

He slipped. He was tired, he was emotional, and as he looked her in the eye, he slipped right into honesty. "Because we both remember that afternoon by the pool, and how much we wanted to date each other. We didn't think friendship would be enough."

Damn, he could kill her smiles without even trying.

"You never wanted to date me, Thane. You should be honest about it." She tossed her patrol cap a few feet in the air, spinning it like a chef with pizza dough. Caught it, tossed it. "It's not a bad thing. It actually makes it easier to work with you, knowing that I'm not your type. You were just flirting with me…recreationally, shall we say? Trying to see if you could get the single girl to believe your lines."

He frowned. "I don't flirt recreationally. I don't flirt at all."

"Oh, but you do. And you were very convincing, but I know that's what you were doing. You said so."

He stepped closer. "Never. I said it was never a game."

She snorted in disbelief and spun her cap in the air, keeping the cap between them, giving herself something to look at instead of him. "You're talking about when we met in the parking lot for our ride-along."

"Yes. I said it was never a game then. I'm telling you the same thing now." He snatched her cap out of the air and leaned in close, so close he could feel the air move when she sucked in a breath. "Chloe Michaels, it was never a game."

"I'm talking about earlier than that. I heard you at the pool. You told a friend that you were just taking what you could get, because there wasn't any other single girl to talk to."

"You are nobody's idea of taking what they can get."

"I was in the bathroom, Thane. I could hear you with your friend. 'Did you see her face? Believe me, if you'd seen her face…' Sound familiar?"

The entire, desperate conversation with Gevahr came back to him in a single burst. He knew exactly what she was talking about.

"My God, Chloe. You heard that?" He shook his head

as he looked at her and remembered those critical minutes when he'd been trying not to get them caught. "I can't believe you ever spoke to me again."

"I wouldn't have. The army didn't give me a choice, did it?" She smiled, a sort of smart-aleck grin, all bravado. "Don't worry. I didn't get a complex over it. I know my face isn't hideous."

"Not even close. You're beautiful."

"Stop. Seriously. I'm just not your style, and I'm cool with that."

"You are exactly my style. Chloe, I was talking to Gevahr."

He knew when that sank in; her smile faded away.

"It was Sergeant Gevahr, and I'd just figured out you were going to be his platoon leader like five minutes earlier. He said he'd been watching us together, and I was so damned afraid I'd just blown your reputation—but you'd had your back to the pool most of the time. He hadn't seen your face. I made him leave before he could."

Her face. He was looking at her beautiful face now, her lips parted, her eyes wide, her attention riveted on him. He'd come closer to her with each word, until she was nearly backed against his wall. They stared at each other, emotions running high. Hot. God, he could kiss her.

He could not.

"I saw you walk away." She glanced upward, replaying the scene in her mind. "You had your towel over your shoulder, and…oh. It was Gevahr, wasn't it?"

He stepped back, because he had to step back. Her cap was crushed in his fist. He wanted to speak, but his throat felt tight, so he nodded.

She took in a shivery breath and dropped her gaze. "You should have told me."

"I didn't know you'd overheard anything."

"You should have told me," she whispered.

He had to touch her. Her cap was in his fist, but with his other hand he reached toward the curve of her cheek—

He forced himself to stop. Touching her face was too intimate. It was a line that couldn't be uncrossed. He touched her lapel instead, straightening it, his fingers touching fire-retardant industrial cloth instead of Chloe's skin.

"I'll tell you now. The truth was, you looked beautiful. Your smile slayed me. When I said I wanted to take you to dinner and a movie, I meant I wanted to spend every free moment I possibly could with you that day and the next day and the next, as far as I could see into the future."

She stayed perfectly still, eyes downcast.

He dropped his hand to his side. "But then I realized we were both MPs."

She burst into motion. She snatched her cap out of his fist and sidestepped him, turning on him so he was the one against the wall. "You walked out on me. Whether you had a good reason with Gevahr or not, you should have doubled back to the party to explain why you'd just walked out on me. I would have understood all the implications if you'd said you were in the 584th. I might even have thanked you for distracting Sergeant Gevahr. But you didn't. You left me there, and I had no idea why. It was—it was—"

"Heartbreaking," Thane said. That was how he'd felt.

"It was humiliating. There is no excuse for that."

He couldn't defend himself. She was right.

She was also waiting for him to say something. "At the time, I told myself there might be more MPs there, so I shouldn't go back. Another MP had already walked by the fence before I talked to Gevahr. But the truth was—"

The truth was, he'd gone back into his safe world with Ballerina, to try to squash his feelings for Chloe before Monday.

"The truth was, I knew we'd be meeting again on Monday. I tried to convince myself that would be enough time for both of us to shrug it off and move on. It wouldn't have been. Then you rode along on Sunday instead." After Drummer had advised her to choose a confrontation instead of a conversation. He shook his head at the memory. At himself. "I botched everything up, Chloe. I'm sorry."

"Well." She pulled herself together as he watched. She simply took in a deep breath and stood up straighter. By the time she breathed out, she was Michaels. Chin up. Gaze direct. Cool and calm. "This has been a very interesting lunch hour. Or three hours. I'm going back to the office. I'll see you tomorrow."

She reached for the doorknob. He placed his palm on the door to stop her. "I don't want to go back to being Carter and Michaels."

"Are you about to say, 'Can't we still be friends?' That's a breakup line, Thane. You can't use it. We never dated."

She was still hurt. He'd caused this woman too much pain, and yet she'd come here today with cookies and her company when he'd needed her most. Tonight, she would spend all night talking to him on their app if he needed her company, even though Drummer had caused her pain, as well. There had to be a limit to how much pain she was willing to take.

"No, we never dated. I was devastated at that pool party when I realized that this—" He looked at her flushed face, her angry eyes, her ballerina hair and her military uniform. God, how he loved her. "When I realized that this wasn't meant to be. I handled it badly. I'm sorry. I will always be sorry. And yes, I'm asking you to be my friend, anyway."

The sound of her angry, shallow breaths was worse than anything she could have said.

"I know it's asking a lot," he said. "I know you had to forgive your other friend, too, after the ballet. Maybe we can only be expected to tolerate a certain amount of offenses against us, and you've hit your limit. But, Chloe…"

He looked into her face with real regret. "But, Chloe, if you could only forgive one man, then I'm jealous that it was him."

She stopped breathing. "You and I are in the army, Thane." It came out as a whisper. "At least with him, there's a chance... But you and I? We could only be friends."

"That's a lot. That's more than I deserve. Can we make this the start of a beautiful friendship?"

Chloe bit her lip at his *Casablanca* quote, but after a long moment, she opened the door, and he watched her walk away.

She hadn't said yes.

Chapter Twenty

Dear Drummer,
I think we should meet.

Chloe hit Send. She refused to watch that blinking cursor, so she went into the kitchen and poured herself a glass of wine. Then she came back to her living room to peek through her vertical blinds. Thane's balcony was empty. The coast was clear.

She went outside to her little patio set and arranged her laptop and her wine on the table.

Why? Drummer asked.

Chloe's heart sank. Why would you ask why? You don't want to meet me any longer?

I do. I'm just wondering why you changed your mind.

She picked up her wine and sat back, trying to imagine what a confident, fun woman would give as her reason. She ignored Thane's balcony so deliberately that, of course, she noticed the second his glass door slid open and he stepped out, concentrating on the phone in his hand.

The thought came to her as an old reflex: *handsome man; hates me.*

Except he didn't.

Her heart tripped in her chest as she watched him—okay, as she devoured him with her eyes. He was still wearing that snug T-shirt, those loose track pants that had fallen so nicely over his perfect, muscular backside. She wondered if his feet were still bare. She wondered if he'd gone back to sleep after she'd left. Wouldn't it be something if he'd chosen to sleep on the couch because the pillows had kept her shape or her smell?

A silly fantasy. But when he'd said he wanted to be friends, he'd also said she was beautiful.

He lifted his hand and waved at her.

She set her wine down a little too abruptly and gave him a quick wave back, then she bent studiously over her laptop, like it held all the answers to the universe.

Perhaps it did.

Why? I want to meet you because I need a hug now and then. I'd like to hear you laugh when I laugh. I'd like to crash on a couch and do nothing with you.

She ran her fingers over the pink and blue words, a friendly blend, a comforting pattern. She said out loud what she could not write: "I want to meet you because you are the only man who could possibly save my heart from Thane Carter."

I don't know if I can, Baby. I'll get back to you on that.

"Oh." Her breath hitched on her disappointment. She looked in Thane's direction. He was looking in hers.

She wasn't going to cry in front of him. She picked up her laptop and her wine, and went back inside.

"You are out of your mind, Lieutenant Carter."

Thane stood at attention before the brigade commander's desk. This full-bird colonel, the highest-ranking military police officer on post, the provost marshal of Fort Hood, was the last man standing between Thane and his chance at happiness.

"You somehow got your CO to sign off on this. You got your battalion CO to sign off on this. But now it's on your brigade CO's desk, and the buck stops here. My answer is no."

Thane did not flinch outwardly. Inwardly, he did not flinch, either. He exploded—but his military bearing did not change.

"What do you have to say, Carter? How are you going to handle that?"

"There is nothing to say except 'yes, sir.' There is nothing to handle. I will continue to obey all lawful orders and execute the mission."

I will continue to delay happiness.

The colonel let the silence go on a good, long while. "Close the door, Carter. Have a seat."

That was a lawful order. Thane obeyed it. It was a rare occasion, a very rare occasion, when a brigade commander sat down for a one-on-one talk with a platoon leader. Rarer still to have the door closed.

"You are one of the sharpest lieutenants I've seen in my career, Carter. You are being sent to the captain's course at the earliest possible date. You have been recommended for company command by your entire chain of command, including me. I'm doing you a favor here. Never give up your life because some girl strikes your fancy. Nothing that goes on in a bedroom is as important as your career."

"I appreciate that, sir."

The colonel sat back in his leather wingback chair. "Good, good—"

"And I would never do something so foolish. That is not the situation here, sir."

The colonel only raised an eyebrow in question.

Thane took that as permission to speak. His best shot at happiness was in the brigade commander's hands, and every word counted.

"My time as a platoon leader will end the day I make captain. There's a five-week gap between that promotion in May and the start of the captain's course in June. Colonel Stephens told me he'd planned to assign me to the battalion

S-3 shop with Major Nord. I'm not derailing that career path, sir. I'm just asking to make that move twelve weeks earlier."

"That's what Colonel Stephens said to you, is it? Guess what he said to me. He asked me to clarify the definition of 'unit' as far as fraternization goes. Two officers in the same company are obviously in the same unit, but he asked if I thought there was enough of a degree of separation if one officer is in a company and the other is on battalion staff. I have a feeling you've brushed up on the details of fraternization, so you know that's decided at the brigade level. Right here, by the man sitting in my chair."

"Yes, sir."

"I've already told you no."

Thane fought the disappointment. June was far away. Missouri was even farther, but he was going to have to make them work.

The colonel wasn't done with him. "I've got another question for you, Carter. Is Lieutenant Michaels going to be able to keep serving as a platoon leader with you when I send you back to the 584th? Should we call her in here to ask?"

Thane had not and would not draw Chloe into it. "I have not said that I'm interested in Lieutenant Michaels, sir. I have not said she's the reason behind my request."

"Don't play games with me. It's obvious you've got the hots for someone in your company, and Phillips and Salvatore aren't it. The only female officer in the 584th is Michaels. She's new. You're the XO, the senior platoon leader. It would be a hell of a lot easier to move her instead of you."

"That would be grossly unfair to her, sir, since none of this is her idea. She doesn't know I've made this request. She'd be rightfully shocked if an order came down that made her move."

"Shocked? You expect me to believe you two haven't already canoodled around and decided it's love?"

Thane came close to laughing at that one, laughing in disgust. "Sir, we barely manage to be polite to one another. We only succeed in being civil about every third day."

The colonel seemed genuinely curious now. "You're going to all this trouble for a woman who doesn't even like you? What do you think the odds are that you'd ever win her over?"

"Optimistically, sir? I'd say about fifty-fifty."

"You're willing to upend your career for a fifty-fifty shot at a woman who may not even like you?"

"There's zero chance of success if I don't try, sir." Thane decided to take a risk and walk that line between disrespectful and bold. "But I can tell you where there is a one hundred percent chance of success. That's the S-3 shop. If I work for Major Nord more than sixty days, he can give me a rating, and I can guarantee I'll have given him nothing to say but good things. It won't hurt my career to add one more good review to my file before I hit the captain's course."

The colonel leaned forward, managing to get in Thane's face without leaving his seat. "Well, that isn't going to happen, Carter. You're not moving to the battalion S-3 shop."

Damn it. Thane had taken one last swing, and missed.

"Because you're moving to the brigade S-3 shop. This week. You've convinced me you aren't being stupid about your career, but I'm keeping my eye on you."

"Yes, sir," Thane answered automatically. The relief was dizzying, the happiness staggering.

"You're dismissed."

Thane stood, amazed he was still steady on his feet. "Good afternoon, sir."

"Before you go, let me make my policy clear. An officer on brigade staff is not in the same unit as a platoon leader in a line company. I've decided there is no conflict of interest there."

"Yes, sir." Thane headed for the door while he still had some semblance of military bearing.

"Oh, and Carter?"

He wiped the smile off his face before turning around. "Yes, sir?"

"Apparently my brigade is full of a bunch of sappy, damned romantics. Everyone seems to think you and Michaels would make a perfect couple. They're all rooting for you."

To hell with it. Thane smiled.

"Yes, sir."

He walked out of the office and down the brigade staff hall, but that was the end of his self-restraint. He slammed out of the entrance door and pulled his phone out of his pocket.

Yes, Ballerina, let's meet. ASAP.

Today, I am desperate for sanity.

Chloe wasn't going to get it.

The entire week had been crazy. Thane had been tapped to move into the brigade S-3 office even though he wouldn't make captain until May. It was a shock to everybody except Thane, apparently. The platoon leaders and platoon sergeants had hastily passed around a card to sign and had taken him to a restaurant in Killeen for a farewell lunch. Sergeant First Class Lloyd had proposed a toast that had choked everyone up.

Then they'd gone back to work. Thane had parked the chair with the squeaky wheel at his empty desk and left her with a rather intense, "I'll see you around, Chloe. I'm not going far."

But he was far, no longer part of the company. No longer part of the battalion. His office wasn't even in her building.

She sat at her desk, alone, and missed him like crazy.

But the craziest thing of all was that, in just a few hours, Drummer was going to become more than just a man stuck in her laptop.

She wasn't ready. She'd tried to stall. I can't get to Austin until Sunday at the earliest.

Then I'll come to you, Ballerina. Give me your address. I'll take you on a picnic. Thursday after work?

It was lucky that Drummer had chosen Thursday, because troops were dismissed at three instead of five every Thursday. Those extra two hours were supposed to be devoted to family time. Hers were going to be devoted to a picnic with Drummer.

She didn't have a thing to wear.

She looked over her civilian clothes, deliberately passing over anything blue or pink. She wasn't going to do that again. She had some pride left, plus enough self-preservation that she'd stopped just short of telling him her address. She'd told him to pick her up outside the complex's swimming pool, a safer area in public. He'd never know which apartment in which of the six buildings was hers, unless she decided to tell him.

Chloe dressed, then went out to her balcony and looked down at the pool. It was as blue as always, but empty. Even in Texas, the water in February was too chilly for swimming. The afternoon was warm, though, seventy degrees. She'd decided her yellow sundress would work with a navy cardigan over it. Her navy ballerina flats were practical for a picnic, but she did not wear her hair in a ballerina bun. She wasn't going to spend an hour on a floral updo again; Drummer had missed his chance to see that. She'd blown her hair dry and left it down.

It was time. She headed down to the pool, perhaps with a bit of military stoicism on her face. That was how she got through nerve-racking occasions, after all. Drummer should understand that she'd fall back on what had always served her well.

She waited outside the pool's chest-high fence and looked

for…someone. Drummer had refused to give her any description of himself. You'll know me when you see me, he'd written.

As she waited, she heard the growl of an engine built for power, excess power for the size of the sports car that held it. Thane's Mustang came in the complex's entrance. Pulled up to the pool.

And parked.

She wanted to die. The last person she wanted to witness this meeting with Drummer was Thane Carter. If Drummer turned out to be someone flaky, it would be humiliating. If she got stood up again, it would be too humiliating to explain why she was standing around in a dress. If Drummer—

Thane got out of his car. It was awful to have such a handsome nemesis. He looked fantastic in a burgundy knit shirt that clung nicely to strong shoulders, to his ripped arms— she did watch the man do push-ups every day at PT, which wasn't exactly a hardship. At least if Drummer turned out to be a creep, she knew Thane would pummel the guy. Of course, so would she, but if Thane got to him first, there wouldn't be much left for her to pummel, more's the pity, and *oh, my God, I am so not normal. What kind of girl thinks like that? What is Drummer going to say when he finds out I'm a soldier and a cop?*

"You look terrific, Chloe."

She pasted on a polite little smile. "Thanks."

She'd been hoping Drummer would hurry up and get here, but now she prayed he'd be late, just late enough to let Thane clear out of the parking lot and head up to his apartment.

Instead of walking away, Thane popped his trunk and took out a wicker suitcase. A picnic basket. He carried it right up to her—no, right past her, and he went in the gate to the pool.

She felt a little dazed, like she had when she'd gotten a concussion once. She was fine, only she was not, and the world seemed a little surreal. She turned to watch Thane as he carried the basket to that table, their table, the little one in the shade, and set it down. He undid the latches and opened it up, and from here, she could see the champagne bottle and the glasses neatly strapped into the lid.

A picnic basket. She should be thinking something significant right now. She knew she should, but it seemed she couldn't think at all as Thane walked back toward her.

He opened the gate again and stopped a little too close to her, his hands in the pockets of his jeans. "Hello, Ballerina."

Her knees buckled.

"Whoa." He was quick, grabbing her upper arm to keep her from falling, but she'd caught herself. She didn't faint. Of course she didn't faint, because she'd never fainted in her life and she wasn't going to start now. She shook off his hand and took a step back.

"It takes some getting used to, I know." He pushed the gate open. "Come and sit down. You're a little pale."

She was numb. Her lips felt numb, her fingers felt numb and tingly, and she let him escort her to the table like she was some fragile flower, a spun-sugar princess who might break.

"At least we know why the app matched us up. Under careers, I checked 'military officer.' You must have, too."

The reminder penetrated the numbness. She was a military officer, not a woman made out of spun sugar.

Instead of sitting down, she squared off with Thane. "What do you mean by saying you know 'it takes some getting used to'? How do you know that?"

He looked, for the first time, serious. Chagrined. He took a breath, ready to explain.

"You knew before I gave you my address yesterday. How long have you known?"

But again, she didn't wait for his answer. "*The Nutcracker.* You were *there*. You were there because you're... Oh, my God. You came, after all." She thought she might choke on the lump in her throat. Her eyes teared up. He'd come, he'd come, and she hadn't been a fool to believe Drummer would come.

The tears gave way to horror. "You came, but you didn't tell me who you were. You—you—you sat next to me in that lobby. You laughed at my pain. Oh, you incredible *jerk*."

She didn't realize her hand was in motion until Thane caught her wrist before her hand connected with his cheek. She gasped, shocked that she'd even tried to slap him.

She'd never felt so emotional, never been so out of control. No military training could prepare her for this horrible, horrible feeling. Her heart had been broken, and the man who'd broken it had sat next to her on the most miserable night of her life while he drank his whiskey.

She looked into those eyes, those same blue and gray irises she'd noticed that night. The same eyes she'd glared at over the roof of a police cruiser. The same eyes she'd laughed with when they'd pranked their platoon sergeants.

Thane closed his eyes and kissed the palm of the hand he'd captured. "I didn't laugh at you. I was as upset as you are now."

He let go of her wrist but clasped her fingers and held her hand as if she were a lady in a historical movie, and he, the gentleman. He kissed the back of her hand. "I didn't know what to do at first, either."

She instinctively tried to pull her hand back. They were in public.

He lowered her hand, but he didn't let go. She watched as he ran his thumb over her knuckles, a caress so innocent, so intimate.

"You kept pretending to be Drummer."

"Your letter. I couldn't ignore it. And I am Drummer."

"You've known for months. I didn't know who I was talking to. All those things I said about my coworker..." Her cheeks felt hot. "I called you arrogant. And things. Are you angry?"

He squeezed her hand gently. "It was a gift, really. What a gift it is, to see ourselves as others see us."

He smiled, looking at her expectantly. He was so handsome when he smiled, she almost forgot why those words sounded familiar. "Did you just quote Robbie Burns?"

"Ay, my online lass likes her Scottish poet."

Chloe's heart pounded. She couldn't sort out all her feelings. She could almost laugh, but she was mortified, too, a little sad that Drummer was not what she'd imagined, perhaps, and amazed that her very best friend all year could be this handsome man before her, an officer she had grudgingly admired even when she didn't want to.

He reached for her other hand and brought both of her hands up to kiss, watching her with those gray-blue eyes as he did.

"Thane, don't." He couldn't kiss her hands. He couldn't kiss her anywhere. She looked over her shoulder to see if anyone was coming up the walk.

"It's safe, Chloe. I did know what to do about that, at least." His smile turned a little devilish, so intimate, her fingers trembled in his. "The brigade commander has made his fraternization policy very clear. He said officers in line companies are free to date brigade staffers."

"He said that?"

Thane smiled at her and raised her hand not to his lips, but to the side of his face, gently drawing her knuckles along his cheek. He must have shaved recently, just for this. Just for her.

"You asked him," she breathed, though it was hard to breathe. "You asked the brigade commander. Oh, Thane, you didn't lose your position because of me?"

"Nope." He winked at her with a little of that arrogance she'd once lied and told Drummer she found unappealing. "I was going to be sent to the battalion S-3, anyway. He just promoted me to brigade S-3 instead and let me start twelve weeks early."

"Twelve weeks." She was absolutely mesmerized by him, by the way his hand felt warm and strong, by the way his mouth formed words, by the way his eyes never, ever left hers. "What do you need those twelve weeks for?"

He let go of her fingers to capture her whole hand and pressed the palm of her hand against the side of his face. "Do you realize we've never touched before?"

"That's not true." Her heart was still pounding, but it was steady. She was getting used to it, breathing through it. "The day we met, we sat side by side right at this pool with our feet in the water. Our feet brushed against each other. I nudged you with my shoulder when you made me laugh."

He looked so tenderly at her, she thought she would melt. "Such a little touch to live on, wasn't it? Such a little touch, but it kept us going for three months, here at Hood. Eight months online. Do you realize you've been my favorite person in the world for eight months?"

She didn't wipe the tears that trickled down her cheeks, because she didn't want to let go of Thane's hands. It was okay to cry a little; only Thane would see, and he would understand why she cried for a silly, wonderful, online love.

"We're really, really good at keeping up a long-distance relationship, Baby. That's a really, really good trait for a military couple to have." He tugged her closer, then let go of one hand so he could slide his arm around her waist and pull her close. The impact was exciting, energizing, awakening a whole new awareness. He felt as hard as he looked during PT, strong arm, hard thighs, but he felt warm and giving, too, a body she could press into, lie upon, rest against.

"But for these twelve weeks?" she asked, smiling against his mouth. Whether he'd brought his mouth to hers or she had to his didn't matter, because the kiss that followed was all she'd ever wanted. Strong, warm, giving—the best first kiss any couple could ever have.

He spoke with his lips against hers. "Now we've got

twelve weeks to get really, really good at being very, very close."

She laughed, they kissed, and he tasted so good and felt so very right, she knew the picnic was going to be eaten either by a red, red couch or in front of a massive TV.

After.

She ran her hand up his neck, sliding her fingers through his short hair. "And what happens at the end of twelve weeks?"

"Then you will be the one who pins the captain's bars on me, and I will be the one who puts a ring on your finger."

There may have been a tear trickling down his cheek as well, but it didn't matter, because only she was here to see it—and she could see nothing while kissing her best friend in the world.

* * * * *

Look for Caro Carson's next book in October 2018!

And for more great military love stories, check out the rest of the AMERICAN HEROES *miniseries:*

CLAIMING THE CAPTAIN'S BABY
By Rochelle Alers

A SOLDIER IN CONARD COUNTY
By Rachel Lee

A PROPOSAL FOR THE OFFICER
By Christy Jeffries

SOLDIER, HANDYMAN, FAMILY MAN
By Lynne Marshall

Available now from Harlequin Special Edition!

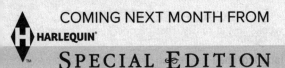

COMING NEXT MONTH FROM

HARLEQUIN®

SPECIAL EDITION

Available May 22, 2018

#2623 FORTUNE'S HOMECOMING

The Fortunes of Texas: The Rulebreakers • by Allison Leigh
Celebrity rodeo rider Grayson Fortune is seeking a reprieve from the limelight.
So as his sweet real estate agent, Billie Pemberton, searches to find him the
perfect home, he struggles to keep his mind on business. Grayson is sure he's
not cut out for commitment, but Billie is convinced that love and family are
Grayson's true birthright...

#2624 HER SEVEN-DAY FIANCÉ

Match Made in Haven • by Brenda Harlen
Confirmed bachelor Jason Channing has no intention of putting a ring on any
woman's finger—until Alyssa Cabrera, his too-sexy neighbor, asks him a favor.
But their engagement is just for a week...isn't it?

#2625 THE MAVERICK'S BRIDAL BARGAIN

Montana Mavericks • by Christy Jeffries
Cole Dalton thought letting Vivienne Shuster plan his wedding—to no one—
would work out just fine for both of them. But now not only are they getting
caught up in a lot of lies, they might just be getting caught up in each other!

#2626 COMING HOME TO CRIMSON

Crimson, Colorado • by Michelle Major
Escaping from a cheating fiancé in a "borrowed" car, Sienna Pierce can't think
of anywhere to go but Crimson, the hometown she swore she'd never return
to. When Sheriff Cole Bennet crosses her path, however, Crimson starts to
look a little bit more like home.

#2627 MARRY ME, MAJOR

American Heroes • by Merline Lovelace
Alex needs a husband—fast! Luckily, he doesn't actually need to be around,
so Air Force Major Benjamin Kincaid will do perfectly. That is, until he's
injured—suddenly this marriage of convenience becomes much more than
just a piece of paper...

#2628 THE BALLERINA'S SECRET

Wilde Hearts • by Teri Wilson
With her dream role in her grasp, Tessa needs to focus. But rehearsing with
brooding Julian is making that very difficult. Will she be able to reveal the
insecurities beneath her dancer's poise, or will her secret keep them apart?

HSECNM0518

SPECIAL EXCERPT FROM

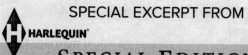

HARLEQUIN

SPECIAL EDITION

*Cole Dalton thought letting Vivienne Shuster
plan his wedding—to no one—would work out just
fine for both of them. But now not only are they getting
caught up in a lot of lies, they might just be getting
caught up in each other!*

*Read on for a sneak preview of
the next MONTANA MAVERICKS story,
THE MAVERICK'S BRIDAL BARGAIN
by Christy Jeffries.*

"You're engaged?"

"Of course I'm not engaged." Cole visibly shuddered. "I'm not even boyfriend material, let alone husband material."

Confusion quickly replaced her anger and Vivienne could only stutter, "Wh-why?"

"I guess because I have more important things going on in my life right now than to cozy up to some female I'm not interested in and pretend like I give a damn about all this commitment crap."

"No, I mean why would you need to plan a wedding if you're not getting married?"

"You said you need to book another client." He rocked onto the heels of his boots. "Well, I'm your next client."

Vivienne shook her head as if she could jiggle all the scattered pieces of this puzzle into place. "A client who has no intention of getting married?"

"Yes. But it's not like your boss would know the difference."

"She might figure it out when no actual marriage takes place. If you're not boyfriend material, then does that mean you don't have a girlfriend? I mean, who would we say you're marrying?"

Okay, so that first question Vivienne threw in for her own clarification. Even though they hadn't exactly kissed, she needed reassurance that she wasn't lusting over some guy who was off-limits.

"Nope, no need for a girlfriend," he said, and she felt some of her apprehension drain. But then he took a couple of steps closer. "We can make something up, but why would it even need to get that far? Look, you just need to buy yourself some time to bring in more business. So you sign me up or whatever you need to do to get your boss off your back, and then after you bring in some more customers—legitimate ones—my fake fiancée will have cold feet and we'll call it off."

If her eyes squinted any more, they'd be squeezed shut. And then she'd miss his normal teasing smirk telling her that he was only kidding. But his jaw was locked into place and the set of his straight mouth looked dead serious.

Don't miss
THE MAVERICK'S BRIDAL BARGAIN
by Christy Jeffries,
available June 2018 wherever
Harlequin® Special Edition books and ebooks are sold.

www.Harlequin.com

USA TODAY bestselling author

SHEILA ROBERTS

returns with a brand-new series set on the charming Washington coast.

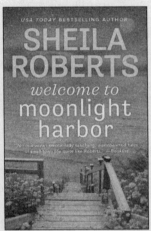

Once happily married, Jenna Jones is about to turn forty, and this year for her birthday—lucky her—she's getting a divorce. She's barely able to support herself and her teenage daughter, but now her deadbeat artist ex is hitting her up for spousal support...and then spending it on his "other" woman. Still, as her mother always says, every storm brings a rainbow. Then, she gets a very unexpected gift from her great-aunt. Aging Aunt Edie is finding it difficult to keep up her business running The Driftwood Inn, so she invites Jenna to come and run the place. The town is a little more run-down than Jenna remembers, but that's nothing compared to the ramshackle state of The Driftwood Inn. But who knows? With the help of her new friends and a couple of handsome citizens, perhaps that rainbow is on the horizon after all.

Available now, wherever books are sold!